CW00552920

The other Monarch of The Glen

peter kerr

Oasis-WERP

Published by Oasis-WERP 2018

ISBN: 978-0-9576586-8-4

Copyright © Peter Kerr 2018

All rights reserved

No part of this book may be reproduced, stored in a retrieval system,
or transmitted in any form or by any means, without the written permission
of the copyright owner. The right of Peter Ker to be identified as the
author of this work has been asserted in accordance with Sections 77
and 78 of the Copyright, Designs and Patents Act 1988.

A catalogue record of this book is available from the British Library.

www.peter-kerr.co.uk

Cover design © Glen Kerr

Typeset by **www.benottridge.co.uk**

ALSO BY THIS AUTHOR

(Non-fiction)

Snowball Oranges

Mañana, Mañana

Viva Mallorca!

A Basketful of Snowflakes

From Paella to Porridge

Thistle Soup

Don't Call Me Clyde!

(Fiction)

The Mallorca Connection

The Sporran Connection

The Cruise Connection

Fiddler on the Make

The Gannet Has Landed

Song of the Eight Winds

ABOUT THE AUTHOR

Best-selling Scottish author Peter Kerr is a former jazz musician, record producer and farmer. His award-winning Snowball Oranges series of humorous travelogues was inspired by his family's adventures while running a small orange farm on the Spanish island of Mallorca during the 1980s. Peter's books, written with warmth, gutsy style and spiky humour, are sold worldwide and have been translated into several languages. He is married, with two grown-up sons, and lives in East Lothian.

www.peter-kerr.co.uk

TABLE OF CONTENTS

CHAPTER ONE

*

EDINBURGH, CAPITAL OF SCOTLAND –
AUGUST 1990

* * * * *

Princes Street had never looked more alluring: a cloudless summer sky, the castle towering on its craggy seat above the glen of gardens that form a backdrop to one of the most spectacular avenues in the world. Yes, thought James McCracken, Princes Street was special. Edinburgh was special – unique, a treasure. And that really meant something, coming from a Glasgow man.

At the corner of Waverley Bridge, a clutch of camera-toting Americans gazed awe-struck at a piper as he skirled the strains of *Scotland the Brave* over a scattering of coins in an upturned bonnet. James, wearing his sixty years well (and knowing it!), smiled a contented smile while he weaved his way through the throngs of tourists trudging up the slope from the railway station. He had enjoyed his visit to Edinburgh, having stopped off briefly en route from London to the Scottish Highlands to take in a little of the cultural atmosphere. Culture was his business, and he liked to 'top up' his stock-in-trade whenever the opportunity arose. The fact that the nearest he'd come to culture on this occasion had been a stand-up comedy gig in a Grassmarket pub mattered not a whit. He'd been in Edinburgh during the International Festival of the Arts and, in due course, would make a point of mentioning this to anyone who might be impressed.

Dressed casually but stylishly in a fine tweed sports jacket and lightweight slacks, James trailed his Louis Vuitton suitcase through the swarms of people coming and going across the station concourse. He paused to buy a copy of *Scottish Field* from the news stand, where he flashed the sales girl a melting smile. It had been said that he bore more than a passing resemblance to Sean Connery. James agreed, and he flaunted it – discriminatingly, of course.

Beneath the main arrivals/departures board, meanwhile, Charlie Skidmore was scanning the information through his sunglasses, a seen-better-days Adidas holdall under his arm, a slightly perturbed expression on his face. Charlie was as macho as they come, but knew from the smirks he was attracting that those around him reckoned he was about as camp as a field full of wigwams. In his mid fifties and looking leaner and fitter than many half his age, Charlie was clad from head to toe in black leather, a studded biker jacket and peaked 'captain's' cap giving him the appearance of a refugee from the Village People pop group. Long, wild hair and a goatee beard added a certain Bohemian quality to his appearance: a look that Charlie had deliberately cultivated over recent years.

He duly made his way to the booking office, where he lined up behind a small, elderly woman who was nervously gathering up her ticket and change at the window. With her bits and pieces finally tucked into her handbag, she turned to leave. Seeing Charlie staring down at her, she caught her breath and clapped a hand to her mouth.

'Oh, my God Almighty!' she twittered. 'The things ye see at Festival time!'

'Aw, relax, granny,' Charlie muttered in a broad Glasgow drawl. 'Ah only eat the under-nineties!'

She bundled him out of the way and toddled off in haste.

'Next!' yelled the ticket clerk.

'Oh, eh, Inverness return, pal.' Charlie cast a despondent glance at the money he was parting with. 'And, ehm, that'll need to be second class, like.'

He was checking his change with an even more disconsolate look when he walked into the crowded station bar a couple of minutes later. Ignoring any derisory reaction to his garb, Charlie took a few moments to survey the scene, wheels turning in his mind. He raised an eyebrow as he noticed the immaculate form of James McCracken sipping a glass of wine at the far end of the bar. Charlie edged his way through the crush until he was standing next to him. Then, faking a shove by one of the nearby scrum of customers, he stumbled into James's shoulder, causing his drink to spill down his jacket.

'Aw, heh, sorry, pal. Ah mean, Ah just got bumped in the…'

'Please don't worry about it,' James replied in a refined Scots accent. He calmly pulled a handkerchief from his top pocket and started to dab his lapels. 'These things happen, and I'm sure it wasn't your –'

'That's right,' Charlie cut in, while flicking the front of James's jacket with his fingers, 'but Ah just hope it'll no stain – know what Ah mean?'

James gave Charlie a reassuring smile. 'It's only white wine. Absolutely no problem.'

'Aye, well … as long as ye're sure and that.'

James took his handkerchief and mopped some drops of wine that had splashed onto Charlie's arm. 'I'm very sure. In fact, the wine's more likely to damage *your* jacket. After all,' he winked, 'we wouldn't want to rust the rivets, would we?'

Charlie feigned a laugh. 'Yeah, right enough! So, no harm done, then, eh?'

As Charlie made to leave, James grabbed his wrist, shook his hand and gave him a hearty slap on the shoulder. 'Think no more of it, friend.'

'Aye, right,' Charlie replied, smiling uneasily as he attempted to free his hand from James's grip. 'Nice meetin' ye. And, uh … all the best, all right?'

With that, he turned tail, elbowed his way through the crowd and left the bar with a self-satisfied smile on his lips. James watched him go, a knowing smile on *his*.

Charlie made a beeline for the gents' toilets, where he nipped smartly into one of the cubicles and locked the door. Breathing hard, he slipped a hand inside his leather jacket and pulled out a wallet – a fat one. A grin of delight lit his face as he surveyed the contents. 'Ya fuckin' beauty!'

But, as Robert Burns once said, 'The best-laid schemes o' mice an' men gang aft a-gley.' And those were the very words quoted by James McCracken as the cubicle door burst open. He still had that knowing smile on his lips. Charlie could only stand open-mouthed as James calmly removed the wallet from his hand.

'Mine, I believe?'

'Aw, heh, listen, pal – Ah never took nothin'. Ah mean, ye can check – there's nothin' missin', like.'

James ran a thumb over the wad of the banknotes. 'Yes, well, everything seems to be tickety-boo.' He put the wallet into his inside pocket, tweaked Charlie's cheek, wished him a pleasant bowel movement, and left.

Gobsmacked and shaking, Charlie slumped back against the cubicle wall. 'Bugger me!' he gasped. 'Ah never saw *that* comin'!' But what was the point in standing there feeling sorry for himself? There was a train to catch. He pulled back the cuff of his jacket to check the time. No watch there. He tried the other wrist. Ditto.

'What the hell…!' Sensing a bad penny poised to drop, he felt the breast pocket of his jacket. 'Nah, it couldnae be!' But it was. He gave the same treatment to his trousers. Ditto.

'Ma bloody wallet! A hundred quid – ma holy all! The lousy, thieving bas–'

He was cut off in mid expletive by a Tannoy announcement: '*The train about to leave Platform Three is the 11.30 to Inverness, calling at Perth, Pitlochry, Aviemore –'*

'Yeah, yeah, yeah!,' Charlie growled, scrambling out of the cubicle. 'Hold yer damn horses! Ah'm comin'! Ah'm *COMIN'!*'

*

As Charlie scurried panting past the Inverness train's first class coaches, he failed to notice James sitting in solitary comfort inside, reading his copy of *Scottish Field*. The guard's whistle blew the very second Charlie clambered up from the platform. But there was nothing solitary about conditions in the second class carriage he found himself in. With the train gathering speed, he ricocheted his way between row after row of full seats, paying no heed to the who's-this-weirdo? glances he was attracting from the broad mix of nationalities on board. And the same situation prevailed in every carriage he passed through. It was the height of the tourist season, and there wasn't a single empty seat available throughout the entire length of the train. Not in the second class parts at any rate.

'Ach, well, at least the view's good,' Charlie grunted, having ultimately resigned himself to slouching against a bulkhead wall outside one of the toilets. Through the window of an adjacent door he could see that they were passing between the cat's cradle of steel that forms the world-famous Forth Rail Bridge. And the view was indeed good. Peering through the network of girders, he could make out every detail of the Firth of Forth, all the way down to North Berwick Law, rising behind the shore like a giant molehill some thirty miles to the east.

But there was still a long journey ahead, and spectacular views weren't going to help take the weight off his feet. On the other hand, the mundane view of a toilet door just might. Or, better still, a glimpse of its 'Vacant' sign actually could. And it did.

Eureka! In a trice, Charlie had locked himself in and was making ready for a rest – his backside on the lavatory seat, his legs splayed out in front, his old holdall serving as a pillow for his head. He leaned back and pulled his cap down over his eyes.

'Ah-h-h-h … it's maybe no five-star, feather-bed luxury, but to my aching arse this is the Presidential Suite in the fuckin' Waldorf Astoria.'

Before long, the steady rhythm of the rails had lulled him to sleep.

*

Back in first class, James McCracken laid aside his magazine as a steward arrived carrying a small silver tray.

'Your dry Martini, sir.'

'Ah, marvellous.' James gave the steward an enquiring smile. 'Stirred, not shaken, I take it?'

'Just as you ordered it, sir.'

'Excellent – thank you!'

James took a sip of his drink, then settled back to admire the passing scenery.

PETER KERR

*

In the interim, a potential state of emergency was developing outside Charlie's toilet. A myopic Japanese couple were standing muttering to each other, while gesturing irately towards the toilet door. They were muttering in English, but with a pronounced Japanese accent. The man finally raised his wrist watch to his wife's face and pointed at the dial. 'Nearly thirty minutes already,' he spluttered. 'Bloody ridiculous!'

His wife was standing with her legs crossed, a pained expression distorting her features. 'Mmm-ee-oo-ee!' she yodelled.

Totally unaware of the drama unfolding only a few feet away, Charlie Skidmore was snoring away blissfully under his cap.

'Oh please, *please* hurry,' the Japanese woman whimpered, looking distinctly distressed, and writhing a bit as she stared rheumy-eyed at the 'Engaged' sign. 'I *absolutely* desperate!'

His patience exhausted, her husband started to bang on the toilet door. 'Open up! Lady need use bathroom! She completely frantic already!'

A string of profanities emanating from within eventually revealed that Charlie had been roused from his slumbers. And he was not amused. 'OK, OK, OK!' he growled. 'Tell her to hold onto her doughnut!'

Charlie opened the door just as the little Japanese man was about to give it another thump. His fist hovered in mid air as he stared up slack-jawed into the darkness of Charlie's shades, while his wife barged past them both and slammed the toilet door behind her. A forefinger unwound itself from the man's still-raised fist and pointed trembling in the direction of her retreat. 'No got doughnut problem,' he quavered through a sheepish smile. 'Got dy-horia-hi-hay!'

*

While all this was going on, James McCracken had repaired to the first class dining car and was sitting at an immaculately-set table, tucking into a succulent steak with all the trimmings. The waiter poured him a glass of red wine.

'Everything to your satisfaction, sir?'

'Absolutely excellent, thank you.' He gestured towards his plate. 'Um, this steak…?'

'Aberdeen Angus, sir.'

James nodded, smiling. 'But of course. Marvellous!'

*

Charlie, cap on the back of his head, had now resumed his former position, standing slumped against the bulkhead by a door. He was gazing glumly out of the window, taking in the magnificent Highland scenery, but in no mood to appreciate it. With a sigh, he dipped his hand into a trouser pocket and pulled out a few coins and four crumpled one-pound notes.

'Stuff it!' he shrugged, 'In for a penny…!' He picked up his holdall and trudged off in the direction of the second class buffet car.

The cramped, smoky bar was packed with chinwagging, guffawing male customers, all swaying to the motion of the train and nearly all pissed, or getting that way. Empty beer bottles and used plastic tumblers littered every horizontal surface, while the floor was a flotsam of spilt drink, dropped peanuts, fag ends and potato crisps.

'Jesus!' Charlie grumped. 'A public shit house with a booze licence!'

As he made his way to the counter, silence fell like a wet blanket on the assembled clientele – eyes on sticks, wisecracks being muttered behind cupped hands. The barman was drying glasses, unfazed and indifferent. He'd seen it all before.

'Help you?' he said to Charlie.

'Yeah, bottle o' beer, pal. Aye, and better gimme one o' yer sandwiches and all, like.'

'Boiled ham do you?'

'Hmm … what else ye got?'

'That's it.'

Charlie gave him a might-have-bloody-well-known-it look. 'Aye, well, better make it the boiled ham, then, eh!'

He leaned both elbows on the counter and stared blankly at the barman while he was fixing his order. After a few seconds, someone in the still-hushed pack behind him started to sing the Village People's *In the Navy*, prompting an eruption of communal laughter. Slowly, Charlie turned round and eyeballed the mickey-taking culprit, a young drunk who was standing at the back of the crowd, gleefully accepting the accolades of two giggling mates. The rest of the customers, meanwhile, were happily resuming the rhubarb of banter that Charlie's arrival had interrupted. For them, the comic interlude was over. But it was only just beginning for Charlie…

The barman tapped him on the shoulder, drawing his attention to the sandwich and bottle of beer he had brought to the counter.

'Four pounds, fifty-five!'

'For *that*?' Charlie retorted.

The barman indicated a price list behind the bar. 'What you ordered, isn't it?'

Mumbling to himself, Charlie shook his head in dismay. He dipped into his pocket, fished out his miserable stash of cash and threw the whole lot onto the counter. 'Keep the bloody change!'

*

In stark contrast, James McCracken was downing the last of his wine in the pampered comfort of the first class dining car.

'Excellent, thank you,' he said to the waiter.

'Something from the sweets trolley, sir?'

'No, um, just coffee, please. Oh, and a cognac – *Hine*, if you have it. Yes, and I'll have a look at your selection of cigars, if I may.'

*

Back in the buffet car, Charlie was still standing at the bar. He took a bite from his sandwich, squirmed, dropped it onto its plate and shoved it away. After taking a slug from his bottle of beer, he grimaced, looked at the label, then said to the barman, 'What the hell's this for a Highland brew – stag's piss or somethin'?'

The barman shrugged, but said nothing.

'Aye, and they reckoned Sid Snot snuffed it with Kenny Everett,' bellowed the young drunk who'd made the Village People connection a bit earlier. He and his mates dissolved into cascades of laughter.

Calmly, Charlie lifted his abandoned sandwich, ambled over and stuffed it into the lad's mouth. 'You and the ham were meant for each other, pal. Enjoy!' As the lad spluttered, Charlie gave his mates a manly slap on both cheeks, posed hand-on-hip, pursed his lips and whispered, 'See yiz at the YWCA, girls!'

At that, he cocked his cap at a jaunty angle and swaggered out of the buffet car, not bothering too much about who he collided with in the process.

* * * * *

CHAPTER TWO

*

AN HOUR LATER – INVERNESS, CAPITAL OF
THE HIGHLANDS…

* * * * *

Outside the station, Charlie looked up at a large sign which read: '*CEUD MILE FAILTE* – A HUNDRED THOUSAND WELCOMES'

As long as they were of the folding variety, he mused, he'd settle for a helluva lot less than that right now.

In the swarm of to-ing and fro-ing travellers, James McCracken was now making *his* way out of the station, following a man in chauffeur's uniform who was carrying his suitcase. Charlie caught sight of them just as James was climbing into a vintage Rolls Royce, parked nearby…

'It cannae be! But it *is*! It's the sticky-fingered wide boy that nicked ma watch *and* ma wallet!' He started to run towards the Roller. 'Heh, you!' he hollered. 'Stop! Gimme back ma hundred quid, ye thievin' piece o'…'

But he was wasting his breath. James was completely oblivious. The fact of the matter was that he didn't even know Charlie had been on the train, and doubtless wouldn't have given a toss anyway. The car glided off, with Charlie left standing on the pavement – puffing, perplexed and penniless.

'…Shite!' he said, in delayed completion of his failed appeal for reimbursement. 'Shite! Shite! *Shite*!'

* * *

The image of sun-lit mountains reflected on the surface of Loch Ness would have lifted the spirits of all but the most morose of souls. And Charlie Skidmore saw himself as a fully paid-up member of that hapless club as he shuffled along the road towards Drumnadrochit. He had only been walking for an hour or so, but already his feet were giving him gyp, and, despite its dearth of contents, that damned old holdall of his felt like it was full of bricks. All the while, a lark was singing high above the roadside heather, its song jarring Charlie's ears like Louis Armstrong on helium. Not that he disliked Louis Armstrong. He was a big 'Satchmo' fan, in fact – but not today, not here, and not doing an impersonation of a bloody skylark.

'What a wonderful world?' he muttered. 'Aye, Ah don't fuckin' think so!'

Most of what little traffic he'd encountered so far had been travelling the other way, so the sight of a juggernaut bearing down on him from the direction of Inverness produced a much-needed ray of hope. Truckers were decent spuds, Charlie reflected – always ready to help a traveller in distress. Not this trucker. And Charlie being dressed like a pansified apology for a Hell's Angel might have been the reason. With twin horns blaring, the truck roared past.

Charlie's lift-thumbing hand closed into a fist, which he brandished in the truck's slipstream. 'Away and stuff yersel', bawbag!' he yelled. 'Aye, and Ah bet the Loch Ness Monster turns out to be yer wife!'

But, when one door closes…

The tooting of a car horn drew Charlie's attention back in the opposite direction, where an open-top Jaguar E-Type was now approaching at speed. Hope springing eternal, out went his thumb again.

Up went the Jag-driver's middle finger as he also roared past, grinning.

Even this fleeting glimpse of the fellow, who was wearing a Barbour cap, shades, checked shirt and a gormless expression, suggested to Charlie that he was a typical Hooray Henry: a chinless-wonder country toff, whose pedigree had long since become devoid of even the slightest trace of hybrid vigour.

'Inbred prick!' was the more succinct analysis offered by Charlie as he bellowed once more into a buffeting slipstream. Yeah, he knew the type well…

* * *

While the chauffeur was fetching his suitcase from the Rolls, James McCracken stared admiringly at the turreted facade of Strathsporran Castle, and marvelled at its lochside location on the lower slopes of Ben Doon. Just then, the sound of a car crunching up the gravelled sweep heralded the approach of a Jaguar E-Type, horn tooting, its Barbour-capped driver waving delightedly.

'Ah, James, you old pirate!' beamed Hamish, Lord Strathsporran, as he swung a leg out of the Jag, exposing a ribbon of snowy skin between the top of his woolly hose and the cuff of his knee-length shooting breeks. 'How a-absolutely magic to see you again!'

'Yes,' James smiled, 'it's been some time – much too long.'

They embraced briefly, then Hamish held James at arm's length, looking him up and down. 'Wow, you're looking bloody – well, er – *fit*, I m-must say, old boy!'

James raised his shoulders. 'Well, you know – a lifetime of clean living.'

Hamish slapped his back and let rip with a silly laugh: 'Hwaar! Hwaar! Hwaar! Yah, I bet you could give me twenty years, yet you'd pass for my twin brother any day.'

James thought it prudent to let that speculation pass without comment. 'Good of you to lay on transport from the station,' he said instead, gesturing towards the chauffeur, who was now lugging his suitcase towards the castle.

'Ah, so Hutchinson was on time, I take it?'

'Absolutely. Took me on a little tour of your estate when we got here too. Very considerate.'

Hamish pulled a that's-what-I-pay-him-for shrug, draped an arm over James's shoulder and ushered him towards the castle entrance. 'So, do tell, old fruit – how are things in London? There's still nowhere quite like the w-wicked old metrollops, don't you think?'

* * *

Down on the main road a short time later, an ancient tractor pulling a trailer laden with straw bales drew up outside the castle gates. Charlie, who had been squatting on top of the load chewing a piece of straw, jumped down, stretched and surveyed the massive wrought iron gates lying open beneath an elaborately-sculptured archway. A sign on one side read: '*STRATHSPORRAN CASTLE – Open to the Public, 10 a.m. to 4 p.m. Daily – Admission £3*'.

'Hard-up bunch, them aristos,' he mumbled to himself. 'Aye,' he smirked, 'but it's all a matter o' degree!'

'This where ye wanted off, son?' shouted the tractor driver, eager to be on his way.

'Aye, this seems to be the place. Thanks, pal.'

Charlie threw him a salute, shouldered his old holdall and plodded off through the gateway. Knackered as he was, it took him a good fifteen minutes to wind his way up the rhododendron-lined drive. But it wasn't the condition of his feet that stopped him in his tracks when he rounded the final bend. He stood, eyebrows arched, as he pondered the E-Type Jag and vintage Roller parked on the castle forecourt.

'Well, how about that?' he muttered, smirking again. 'It's a true sayin' – ye never know what's round the corner!'

19

He continued on and climbed the stone stairway to the main door, yanked the bell-pull and took a couple of steps back to gaze up at the towering splendour of castle. 'Quite a pad, Charlie boy!' he nodded. 'Yeah, quite a fuckin' pad!'

The heavy wooden door creaked open and a stern-looking man dressed in butler's garb appeared. He did a double-take at Charlie. 'Yes!' he barked, clearly unimpressed by what he was looking at.

'Right, zero hour!' thought Charlie. 'Better give this pompous old arsehole the *full* fairy treatment!' He assumed the hand-on-hip stance he'd employed when wiping the smiles off the faces of those three young drunks on the train. Pouting, he batted his eyelashes. 'Oh, hi there, sunshine,' he lisped through a coy smile, his Glasgow accent only just discernible now. 'Is, um – well, is Lord Strathsporran about? He, eh, asked me to –'

The butler silenced him with raised hands and lowered brows. 'Do you have an appointment … *sir*?'

'Yes, well, that's just what I was…' Charlie started to fumble in the pockets of his leather trousers. 'Fiddlesticks!' he tutted. 'Can't seem to get it out!' He tilted his head and gave a girly giggle. 'Story of ma life!'

'Get to the point!' snapped the butler.

Charlie struck a shocked pose. 'Oo-oo-ooh! Bit suggestive that, I *must* say!'

*

IN THE CASTLE DRAWING ROOM,
MEANWHILE…

James and Hamish, Lord Strathsporran, were lounging in well-sat-upon Chesterfield chairs by an open fire, nursing drams of whisky. Although sporting a fair range of antiques, the room had a distinctly forlorn look, made all the more dreary by a long line of Hamish's ancestors staring down haughtily from the oak-panelled walls.

James downed the last of his whisky, then stood up and rubbed his stomach. 'Excellent drop of malt, Hamish. Best aperitif of them all, I always say.'

'Couldn't agree m-more, old chap.'

'Now, if you'll excuse me, I think I'll go and freshen up before…'

'Ah, *dinner*! Yes indeed. I was so enjoying your company I almost forgot.' Hamish tittered nervously as he got to his feet. 'Oh, and there's another thing I almost forgot … yes, I have some rather – how can I put it? – well, *interesting* house guests I'm just d-dying for you to meet.'

'Really? Can't wait.'

'Hmm, yah – shooting parties, actually.'

James laid down his glass and patted Hamish on the shoulder. 'Two of my favourite pastimes.'

Patently puzzled, Hamish tugged at his earlobe. 'Two, er … *pastimes*?'

'Yes, you know – shooting and parties.'

Hamish tugged at his other earlobe. The eventual dropping of the penny was accompanied by an explosion of laughter. 'Hwaar! Hwaar! Hwaar! Oh, hey – very droll, James. Yah, bloody brilliant, mate!'

As James left the room by one door, someone knocked at another.

'Come!' Hamish shouted. The butler entered. Hamish glanced up from the fresh glass of whisky he was pouring. 'Yes, Farquharson – what is it?'

'There is a Mr Charles Skidmore to see you, sir.' The butler walked forward and handed Hamish a business card.

A frown furrowed Hamish's brow. 'Interior Design Consultant? Skidmore? I don't know anyone called –'

'Forgive me for interrupting, sir, but he gave me this letter, which, *apparently*, was sent by you. To do with providing estimates for redecorating the –'

'Ah-*hem*!' Hamish coughed. 'Hmm, yes, I do recollect something about … but, er, t-tell him I'm busy, Farquharson.'

'As you wish, sir.' The butler cleared his throat. 'But your letter does mention that he would be welcome to stay … overnight, sir.'

'*What*? Oh … did it? Well, um, ah…' Hamish was getting into a proper flap.

The butler, meanwhile, remained unflappable. 'Shall I show him to the former nanny's quarters, sir?'

Hamish was tugging at both earlobes now. 'Yes, that should – yes, whatever, whatever.' He freed one hand to make a dismissive gesture. 'Just – just carry on, Farquharson!'

The butler bowed a stiff little bow and walked regally to the door, where he turned and cleared his throat again. 'Will Mr Skidmore be joining you for dinner, sir?'

*   *   *   *   *

CHAPTER THREE

*

STRATHSPORRAN CASTLE – EVENING OF
THE SAME DAY

*   *   *   *   *

The castle drawing room was buzzing with conversation as Hamish and his wife Sarah entertained their colourful assortment of house guests to pre-dinner drinks. Everyone was togged up in evening dress, appropriate to individual taste and nationality.

Hamish, resplendent in tartan trews and scarlet mess jacket, was stationed near the door, doing his best to appear at ease while listening to the fractured English of the Japanese couple from the train, now seemingly recovered from their lavatorial ordeal. As luck would have it, their erstwhile adversary Charlie was conspicuously absent from the scene. At the other side of the room, James was standing by the fire, talking to Sarah, Lady Strathsporran, a not unattractive but typically horsey gal in her late thirties. Only a blind man could have failed to notice that she was besotted with everything about her charming companion, not least his kilt and associated Highland accoutrements. And, judging by the general exchange of nods and winks, her fascination certainly hadn't gone unobserved by the other guests present: notably two mature American couples and a pair of middle-aged Italian smoothies.

A few minutes later, the door opened and the butler appeared. 'Ah-*HUM*!' he ejaculated, successfully attracting the weary-eared Hamish's attention.

'Ah, yes, Farquharson. Good man. I – I take it my presence is, um, required elsewhere, is it?'

Ignoring that piece of wishful thinking, Farquharson stuck his chest out in preparation for a ceremonial bellow: 'MY LORD, MAY I PRESENT...' He inserted a butlerly pause, then half turned towards the open door and beckoned with a sideways jerk of his head. '... *MISTER* CHARLES SKIDMORE!'

For the second time that day, a hush descended like a wet blanket as Charlie minced in, still clad in leather, his only concession to formal wear the absence of his 'captain's' cap and the addition of a chiffon scarf knotted round his neck. Camping it up shamelessly, he stopped in front of Hamish and offered a limp hand.

'Submissively at your service, Lord Strathsporran.'

While a spark of recognition flickered in Hamish's eyes, the Japanese couple swapped shocked glances. Over by the fireside, James raised an eyebrow, scratched his nose to mask a smile, then resumed his chat with Sarah.

Hamish was straining to retrieve something from the back of his mind. 'H-how do you do?' he said to Charlie. 'Um, didn't I...? Weren't you on –?'

'I do very nicely, thanks,' Charlie cut in, his expression giving nothing away as he made eye contact with James for a split second. 'Sorry I arrived a bit later than expected this afternoon, your Eminence,' he continued. 'Had to wait *ages* for a taxi at the station.'

Just then, the Japanese couple stepped forward and scrutinised Charlie's face. 'You – you toilet person!' the man frowned.

Charlie shook his head. 'Nah, that'd be a plumber you're after, luvvy. Not my line of business, Mr ehm… '

'Oh, s-sorry,' Hamish flustered. 'How rude of me. This is Mr and Mrs Harikoto, and this is Mr Ska– Ska–'

'Skidmore,' Charlie prompted.

'Quite. And, um, Mr and Mrs Harikoto are from T-Tokyo, you know.'

'Harry … Mrs Koto,' Charlie smiled. 'Pleased to meet you.'

Mr Harikoto's frown deepened. 'Name Harikoto! No Harry … Koto!'

'Yeah, well, I'll have to think about that one, Harry.' Charlie handed him a business card. 'Just let me know if you ever need your sampan touched up. Size no object.'

Mr Harikoto scowled at the card, then handed it back. 'I no read English!'

'Well then,' Charlie shrugged, 'there's no point in buying *you* a subscription to *Gay Times* for Christmas, is there?'

Hamish almost choked on his drink. He swiftly laid a hand on Charlie's arm. 'Gosh, how remiss of me!' he wheezed. 'You haven't got a… Let's find you a s-snifter.'

He turned to the Japanese couple. 'I say, please excuse, will you? I must take Mr Ska– Ska–'

'Skidmore. That's Charles to my friends.'

Hamish responded with an edgy titter, then motioned Charlie to lead the way into the room.

After a few steps, Charlie stopped to look coquettishly over his shoulder. 'So, that'll be Charles to you … I hope.' Paying no heed to the nonplussed glances of the other guests, he sashayed onwards.

While Hamish was taking a discreet but approving eyeful of Charlie's tight-across-the-arse leather pants, Charlie was doing likewise to the rear end of a young woman bending over a coffee table up ahead. She was wearing a French maid's outfit, and Charlie couldn't resist the urge to give her bum a surreptitious pinch as he squeezed past. Although this provoked a little squeal, the maid's look of indignation melted the moment she whirled round to confront the culprit. Charlie could tell she liked what she saw, and he confirmed his reciprocation with a wink.

'Ah, Senga! Just who I was looking for,' Hamish declared. 'A drink for Mr, um-ah…'

'Charles,' said Charlie.

'Quite,' said Hamish. 'Champagne, Senga – for the gentleman!'

Charlie looked smoulderingly into the maid's eyes as he took a glass of bubbly from her tray. 'Bottoms up … Senga.'

She gave him a come-hither smile. 'Any time … sir.'

Hamish was clearly confused, and perhaps a tad upset, by this fleeting flirtation. 'Yes, that'll be all, Senga,' he said with a backwards flick of his hand. 'The, um, other g-guests!'

While the maid wiggled off, Charlie ogled on, prompting Hamish to plant an attention-retrieving hand on his shoulder. 'Now, let me see, Mr… er, *Charles*. Who shall I introduce you to first?'

Without waiting for Hamish to make up his mind, Charlie headed straight for the fireplace, where James and Lady Sarah were sharing a laugh – James being debonair, Sarah acting like a star-struck schoolgirl. Charlie's presence was greeted with a poker-faced look from James, a reaction which his adversary readily mirrored.

The stand-off was relieved by the arrival of Hamish. 'Ah, there you are,' he panted, placing a hand on Charlie's shoulder again. 'Please permit me to introduce my w-wife Lady Stra–'

'*Do* just call me Sarah,' Sarah butted in, exuding cordiality as she extended a hand. 'Welcome to Strathsporran, Mr…'

'Skidmore – Charles Skidmore.' Charlie bowed with all the extravagance of a pantomime principal boy. 'Interior design for the connoisseur.'

James allowed himself a smile: a discreet smile, but a knowing one all the same.

'Golly!' gushed Sarah. 'For the connoisseur, ay? How tremendously exciting!'

Hamish now proceeded to include James in formalities. 'Do you know – I mean, have you met, um…?'

'Mr Skidmark? Not as I recall.'

'Ah, well, do allow me… Charles, this is James McCracken. And James, please meet Charles, er, Skidmark.'

'That's Skid*more*,' Charlie cautioned. 'The Skidmarks were another branch of the family – in the laundry business.'

Confused, Hamish tugged at his earlobe as Charlie and James shook hands, saying nothing, but sparring mentally.

'Wow!' beamed Sarah, drawing on her well-honed skills of melting the social ice. 'Isn't it a coincidence, James? I mean, you know – you being in the art business and everything, and Mr Skidmore being, as it were, a – a –'

'A painter himself?' James suggested.

'Mmm,' Sarah nodded. 'Precisely.'

'Our two professions may indeed have a lot in common,' James concurred. He shot Charlie a taunting smile. 'Wouldn't you agree, my friend?'

Charlie elected to remain silent.

Ever the consummate hostess, Sarah plunged promptly into yet another conversational hiatus. 'So, um, Charles, you're an artist yourself, are you? I say, how completely fascinating!'

Charlie, well aware that James was watching him closely, made a conscious effort not to appear like a cornered rabbit. 'Yes, well, I do – I do paint a bit, yes.'

'Hmm,' James muttered, 'but mainly doors, huh?'

All Charlie could offer in response was a withering look, which triggered a further pregnant silence.

Now it was Hamish's turn to put his inherent grasp of etiquette to good use. 'Hwaar! Hwaar! Hwaar!' he guffawed. 'Oh hey, d-dashed droll, James! *Doors*, huh? Yah, damned witty, old chap!' He nudged Sarah with his elbow, cueing her to join in the hilarity, even if she didn't get the joke. Which she didn't. She let rip with a blast of jolly-hockeysticks giggling anyway.

Charlie could only dredge up an apology for a smile, while silently conceding another round to James. 'But my day will come,' he said to himself. 'Aye, my day will come, ye smarmy bastard!'

With that, a gong rang, and the butler reappeared at the door…

'DINNER IS SERVED, MY LORD! DINNER IS SERVED!'

* * *

THE GREAT HALL OF THE CASTLE – AFTER DINNER THAT EVENING

Although the hall was furnished in Scots-baronial style, and with many period features still intact, a rather shabby quality was nevertheless evident in its general appearance. Beneath the vaulted stone ceiling, Hamish was seated on a throne-like chair at the head of a long, candelabra-lit table. In keeping with convention, the male and female members of his guest list were placed alternately along either side. Everyone was chatting convivially, while Farquharson the butler and Senga the maid circled the table dispensing liqueurs and coffee.

Amid all the ambient bonhomie, however, any sharp-eyed observer would have noticed that certain members of the company had matters other than polite chit-chat on their minds. Hamish, for instance, could frequently be noticed stealing admiring glances at Charlie, while Sarah was similarly targeting James. In the meantime, James was keeping a discreet eye on Charlie, who in turn was taking full advantage of ongoing conversational preoccupations to surreptitiously weigh up a dazzling array of silverware in an adjacent display cabinet.

The wail of bagpipes striking up jolted Hamish from his musing…

'Ah, the pibroch!' he proclaimed, as the notes of a tuneless dirge drifted in through the doorway. 'Magnificent!'

'Oo-oo-ooh!' squealed Sarah. 'How super!'

To the bewilderment of most of their guests, but with the notable exception of James, the host and hostess began to applaud keenly, heralding the slow-marching entrance of a boozy-looking old piper in scruffy, ill-fitting Highland gear. He came to a halt behind Hamish and continued to fumble his way through a seemingly endless piece of melancholy. Hamish, eyes closed, appeared to be in seventh heaven while he finger-mimed the notes on an imaginary chanter. For her part, Sarah adopted a practised air of enthralment, although clueless as to the merits or otherwise of the piper's performance.

Eventually, Homer, one of the American men, reached round in front of his wife and tapped Charlie's hand.

'Hey, what happened, buddy? Somebody in the family just died or somethin'?'

Charlie replied with a non-committal shrug, being more interested in groping Sarah the maid's backside as she leaned over to pour Homer's wife a coffee. Sitting directly opposite, an intrigued James couldn't help but notice Senga throwing her assailant a that's-naughty-but-I-like-it glance, before whispering something in his ear as she moved away. Charlie eyed her departure with obvious approval, and was even more pleased when he spotted a bunch of keys dangling from her waist. Wheels started to turn in his mind again.

As soon as the piper had squeezed the last tortured squawk from his pipes, Hamish started to applaud, with Sarah promptly following suit. For the sake of politeness, a few of the foreign guests made a token attempt at participating in this show of appreciation. The others simply sat in awe-struck silence.

'Bravo, McClung!' Hamish called out. 'Tremendous interpretation, a-as usual!'

Just then, the butler, carrying a silver goblet, appeared gravely at McClung's side.

'Ah, good man, Farquharson!' Hamish beamed. 'The piper's dram!'

McClung raised the goblet to his lips and began to gulp down the contents, while Hamish led the gathered company in a ritual slow hand-clap, followed by a cheer as the last drop of whisky was drained. The old piper belched gloriously, handed the goblet back to the butler, then bowed to Hamish.

'God bless ye, yer – yer Lorship,' he slurred.

'And – and God bless you too, McClung. Yes, an absolutely *exemplary* pibroch, a-as ever!'

Sarah started to applaud again. 'Hear, hear! Absolutely! Well done, er, McClung!'

Hamish, sensing that this was one lily that didn't require any more gilding, swiftly cut her off...

'Ah, now, my dear, I – I think, if you would lead the ladies to the drawing room, we gentlemen shall, um ... cigars and port...'

Hamish stood up, immediately followed by James, and then, gradually and in some confusion, by the other male guests, who were clearly not conversant with this form of post-prandial protocol. Their female partners, equally baffled, duly rose from the table and were shepherded towards the door by Sarah. Right on cue, and in strict compliance with tradition, McClung screwed his pipes back into action and played them on their way with a somewhat wobbly rendition of an old Highland air.

* * *

THE CASTLE DRAWING ROOM – LATER THAT EVENING...

The gentlemen had now joined the ladies. Although the effects of a long, boozy night were beginning to show on some guests, Farquharson and Senga continued to dispense whisky and brandy to anyone still up for it. Taking advantage of the 'relaxed' atmosphere, James, still remarkably sober, slipped unnoticed from the room. He lifted the phone from a hall table, double-checked that no-one was around, then dialled a number…

'Hello, can I speak to Inspector Brodie, please? … Just tell him it's Big Jim – he'll know … Hi, Bill. How are you? … Look, sorry to bother you so late, but have you anything on a guy called Skidmore? That's Charles Skidmore … Yes, I'll hold on.'

He stood whistling quietly for a couple of minutes, then smiled as his contact came back on the line. 'Yes, that's him to a tee … Thanks, Bill – that's all the info I needed. I owe you one!'

Back in the drawing room, Sarah zeroed in on James the moment he came through the door. She'd obviously missed him and couldn't wait to hog his company again. Across the room, Hamish was chatting up Charlie, and making no bones about the fact that he fancied him strongly. But Charlie was more interested, for the present at least, in collaring James about the hundred quid and wristwatch he'd nicked from him in the train station toilets.

'So, Charles,' said Hamish, 'if you'd like to stay another n-night or three, once you've – after you've –'

'Look, sorry, Hamish love,' Charlie butted in, 'but I must have a swift pow-wow with someone, if you don't –'

'Ah, James!' Hamish interjected, waving. 'The very man I wanted to… Um, please excuse, Charles. Do, ah, do have another drink.'

'Well, that was a fuckin' brief courtship!' Charlie muttered to himself as Hamish departed in haste. 'Beaten to the punch again, Charlie boy!'

Hamish grabbed James by the elbow and, leaving Sarah standing open-mouthed and miffed, whisked him away to a quiet corner of the room. James appeared totally at ease, but Hamish was nervy.

'The, uh, painting,' he whispered, glancing furtively around.

Affecting puzzlement, James gave him a come-again look.

Hamish lowered his voice still further. 'You know – on the phone last week, I m-mentioned…'

James faked a light-bulb moment. 'Ah, yes – a picture you wanted me to see, wasn't it?'

'Absolutely. I – I didn't like to… I mean, I didn't want to to be rude by troubling you about business tonight, when you're one's dinner guest. But, um…'

It was obvious to James that Hamish was feeling extremely uncomfortable about broaching the subject of whatever business he had in mind. But business was business, and it had to be encouraged. 'Please, Hamish, do feel free to go on,' he said as sympathetically as he could. 'Whatever you say will be kept strictly between ourselves, I assure you.'

'Oh, what a brick, matey! Marvellous! Yes, it's just that, well, I'm rather keen to –'

He stopped short when, out of the corner of his eye, he noticed Homer the American staggering towards them. Grinning, glass in hand, loud tartan jacket hanging off his shoulders, he slapped Hamish on the back. 'Thanks a million, my, uh – your, um… Say, what the hell does a guy call you anyway?'

Hamish opened his mouth to speak, but Homer got in first. 'Well, hi there,' he said to James, focusing. 'I'm Homer – Homer W.B. McNab – the Third. Yeah, W.B. – that's for Bruce 'n' Wallace, ya know.'

'McCracken – James McCracken. We met earlier, I think.'

'We did?' Homer focused harder. 'Aw, shoot! So we did at that!' He looked at his glass and shook his head. 'Boy, this Scotch! Jesus H!'

James offered a wry smile. 'Yes, after the wine at dinner – the grape and the barley – it can be a lethal mixture, if you're not –'

'Kick-ass rocket fuel, Jimbo!' Swaying, Homer redirected his attention to Hamish. 'Hey, Dook, what NASA wouldn't give for a tankful, huh? Woo-oo-oosh!' He made an upward thrust of his fist, laughed and farted. 'Houston, we have a problem!'

Hamish forced a polite titter.

Just when it seemed that Homer was at risk of making a crash landing, his wife approached, looking suitably embarrassed. 'Gee, Ah'm sorry, Lord Strathsporran. Ah guess Homer is –'

'He's having a *splendid* time,' Hamish interrupted, making a brave attempt at appearing the charitable host, 'and that, Mrs, er, is what we all want, isn't it?'

'Yup, bet your plaid pants we do,' agreed Homer, breaking wind again.

His wife took him by the arm. 'Time for bed, Homer.'

'*Huh*? Aw, hot damn, Millie honey, what the hell's the big rush? Party's only gettin' revved up here. Ain't it, Dook?'

Hamish took a deliberately conspicuous look at his watch. 'Well, my goodness, is that the time? And, uh, we *do* have an early start tomorrow.'

'Sure do,' Millie nodded. 'And thanks again, Lordship. It's been a real swell evenin'.' She elbowed Homer in the ribs. 'Say goodnight, Homer.'

'G'dnight – *hick*! – Homer. See ya in the mornin'.'

By now, the other guests were finishing their drinks too. Sarah was standing by the door, shaking hands as they left and wishing them sweet dreams. Among the last to leave was Bruno, one of the Italian men. With a wolfish smile, he took her hand and raised it to his lips.

'Bee-oo-tiful-a lady. *Mmmwah*!'

'Oo-ooh!' Sarah gasped. 'How gallant!'

Still holding her hand, Bruno fixed her in a simmering stare. '*Contessa – mille grazie. Bella, bella notte*! Wonderful-a food!'

As Bruno kissed her hand again, Sarah went weak at the knees. 'Gosh! How – how kind. Cook *will* be pleased.'

Bruno swept that irrelevance aside with a flood of Latin bullshit. 'Scotland, I love-a the food. But,' he frowned, 'the *cornamusa* – how you say, the bagpeeps? – for me, crap!' His expression morphed into one of approval. '*Si*, but-a your haggises...' He lowered his eyes to survey Sarah's heaving bosom, then kissed his fingertips. '*Uh*! *Fantastico*! *Magnifico*!'

'I say!' said Sarah, flummoxed, but flattered. 'Who *ever* would have thought?'

Over by the fireplace, Charlie was standing where Hamish had left him, still no further forward as regards retrieving his hundred quid from James, though otherwise feeling pretty chuffed with himself. The wheels that had been turning in his mind during dinner were now about to mesh into gear. Or so he hoped.

He watched Senga the maid carrying a tray of glasses towards the door, where she hesitated, glanced over her shoulder and flashed him a wink. Charlie winked back, an impish little smile spreading over his face as he downed the last of his drink.

*　*　*　*　*

CHAPTER FOUR

*

A SHORT TIME LATER – HIGH WITHIN A TURRET OF THE CASTLE

* * * * *

From an alcove in a deserted corridor, the intertwined shadows of a man and woman were being cast by flickering candle light onto the opposite wall. A series of grunts, groans, gasps and whimpers grew steadily louder, reaching a crescendo with a woman's screech…

'NOW! OH, NOW, NOW! OOYA-A-A-A-H!'

A man's voice joined in: 'YES! YES! ARGHH! YA-ESS-SS-SS-AH!

Rhythmic puffing, panting and wheezing ensued, gradually diminishing until the shadowy figures finally slumped apart, exhausted.

'Christ! That was great!' Senga warbled. 'And them all thinkin' you're a fairy and that, Mr Skidmore.'

Charlie chortled, all effeminate posturing banished, for the moment at least. 'Aye, well,' he said, 'there's no many fairies wi' a magic wand like this one, hen.'

Senga started to snigger, but stopped abruptly at the sound of a door creaking somewhere below. A few moments later, the elongated shadows of two men could be seen coming up the turret's spiral staircase. One of them was speaking, his voice muffled, but just discernible…

'So, um, do take care. Rather tricky, these old s-steps, James.'

'Aw shit, it's the boss!' Senga hissed. 'He'll fuckin' kill me!' She grabbed Charlie's arm and nodded towards the opposite end of the corridor. 'Quick! There's another stair along there!'

Charlie was thinking fast. 'Nah… Look, just you mosey along, doll. Ah'll, ehm, Ah'll just hang about here a wee bit longer, OK?'

'Suit yersel', china. Ah'm outta here!'

Senga tiptoed quicksmart away, leaving Charlie free to take a gander at the bunch of key's he'd swiped from her belt. 'Aye, and thanks for the knee-trembler and all, darlin'!' he smirked, then slipped back into the alcove and blew out the candle.

'Phew! Quite a climb!' gasped Hamish as he and James emerged at the top of the stairs.

'Uh-*huh* – and an unusual place for an art gallery, I must say!'

'Ah, but it's hardly that, a-as you'll see.' Hamish took a key from his pocket and unlocked a door diagonally across from where Charlie was lurking. He led James into a small, unfurnished room, lit by a naked bulb dangling from the ceiling. Old trunks, suitcases, box-files, piles of books, a couple of moth-eaten hunting trophies and a variety of other odds and ends littered the floor. The walls were bare, save for a curtained-off area at the back of the room.

'This is what my father called his glory hole,' Hamish revealed. 'Bit of a dump, I'm afraid.' He went on to explain that it was only after his father's death, two weeks earlier, that he'd come into this room for the first time. 'No-one was ever allowed in. I found the key – just by chance, you know. Mmm, hidden away in a drawer of the desk in his study, a-actually.'

While Hamish reflected on that, James took a moment to look around. 'And … the painting?'

'Ah, yes – yes, of course! Forgive me, I was day dreaming there.' Hamish signalled James to follow him over to the back wall. 'Develishly difficult to find the dashed draw string,' he grunted, groping at one side of the curtain.

Charlie, meanwhile, edged from the cover of his alcove and crept over to the side of the open door, where he flattened his back against the wall, ready for a good old eavesdrop.

'Now,' he heard Hamish say, 'If I can just find the – *ouch*! – the confounded light switch. Ah, that's got him!'

Inside the room, James and Hamish were now gazing into a recess that had been concealed behind the curtain. It was empty, apart from a large, gilt-framed painting on the wall, and a solitary chair positioned directly in front. Grubby though the canvas was, James's curiosity was immediately aroused. The subject of the painting was a hairy, long-horned Highland cow, standing regally before a backdrop of magnificent mountain scenery. The animal's pose and the overall composition of the picture struck an instant chord with James. Hamish watched as he produced a small magnifying glass and painstakingly examined several details of the painting, ultimately concentrating on the lower right-hand corner.

'Landseer?' he murmured. '*Can* it be…?'

Without saying anything, Hamish took a faded letter from his jacket and passed it over, his hand trembling.

James's eyes grew wider as he scanned the age-yellowed paper. He looked incredulously at Hamish. 'The royal coat of arms? Surely not…'

'I – I found it tucked into the back of the frame, so…'

James redirected his attention to the letter. 'And it's signed … what's this?'

'Victoria R,' Hamish blurted out, beside himself with anticipation. 'A-and look – the date – 10th September, 1877.'

James nodded his head slowly. 'The year of Queen Victoria's Golden Jubilee. Well, I'll be…'

'Quite,' said Hamish, pointing. 'A-and if you read that bit, you'll see that she'd just spent a weekend here – the guest of one's great grandfather. Yes, and –'

'And she gave him this painting … by Mr Landseer, it says here.' James scratched the back of his head. 'As a small token of her gratitude. Well, I never!'

Hamish could hardly control his excitement now. He pointed at the letter again. 'Yes, and look – just there – she says he'd painted this as a *model*, as she puts it, for –'

'For his wonderful … *Monarch of the Glen* masterpiece.'

'Which, I believe, jolly old Queen Vicky had hanging in Balmoral a-at the time.'

James whistled through his teeth. 'Well, what do you know…?'

Out in the corridor, Charlie's eyes lit up.

Inside the room, James's eyes were drawn back to the painting. 'Damn it, it's uncanny,' he chuckled, 'but true.'

'You really think so?' Hamish checked, scarcely able to contain himself.

'Look for yourself – replace the cow with a stag, and everything else is identical.'

Hamish smiled a sheepish smile. 'Hmm, well, I'll, um, I'll have to take your word for that, old boy. Must confess I'm not too up on *les beaux-arts*, a-as it were.'

James continued to gaze in wonder at the painting. 'And you say it's been locked away in here since…?

'Since 10ᵗʰ September, 1887,' Hamish shrugged, 'for all I know.'

'Extraordinary,' said James absently. He was deep in thought now. 'But yes,' he said at last, 'there *was* a story, if I remember correctly – a legend, almost – that Landseer had painted, well, a *companion* to the *Monarch of the Glen*, but no-one really believed it.' He stroked his chin while continuing to look admiringly at the picture. After a few pensive moments, he turned to Hamish. 'And, ehm … who *else* knows about this?'

Hamish shrugged again. 'No-one. Oh, except the insurance bods, of course.'

'*Insurance*? You mean, your father actually –'

'Absolutely. The policy was stashed away at the back of the frame as well. Hmm, he'd had it valued quite recently too, a-as it happens.'

James gave a little cough. 'So, uh, dare I ask…?'

'Oh, just the round three – er, three m-*million*, that is.'

Out in the corridor, Charlie's mouth reacted without waiting for guidance from his brain. 'Fuckin' arseholes!' he spluttered.

James spun round, startled.

But Hamish couldn't have been less concerned. 'Nothing to worry about. This old place, you know – full of strange noises. Hey, probably just a rat – or a g-ghost!'

Though not entirely convinced, James resumed his appraisal of the painting, but with a more calculating eye now. 'So, if you don't mind my asking, Hamish – what do you intend to do with this?'

Of a sudden, Hamish was struck by an attack of coyness. 'Ah, well, that – that's what I…'

'Come on, Hamish. As I said before, whatever you tell me will go no further.'

'Yah, of course, absolutely, mate. OK, so what I wanted to talk to you about – confide, as it were – is dashed delicate, a-as it happens.' Hamish lowered his head and mumbled, 'Family name and all that, you know.'

'Sorry – don't quite follow.'

Hamish took a deep breath and rushed headlong into what he had to say next: 'Look, James, one has to – one is obliged to – one is forced to…'

'Yes?'

Another deep breath: 'Flog it!'

James feigned surprise. '*Sell* … the painting?'

Crestfallen, Hamish nodded the affirmative.

'But what's wrong with that?' James breezed. 'Should fetch a tidy sum at auction. Believe me, once word gets out that a lost Landseer has been –'

'Ah, but,' Hamish piped up, 'that's just the trouble.'

'Trouble?'

Hamish started to pace slowly up and down what little floor space was available. 'To be perfectly frank,' he said, wringing his hands, 'it's just that one can't sell it, well … *openly.*'

This puzzled James, but he thought it prudent to keep shtum. He sensed a breast being prepared for cleaning. And he sensed right.

After a few more seconds, Hamish stopped and wheeled round. He was in a proper tizz, but a head of steam had been built up and there would be no stopping him now. 'Look, James, there's no point in beating about the bush, OK? I may as well admit it – I'm skint, right? No, worse than that – I'm on the brink of b-bankruptcy. I mean, why do you think one opens one's house to the – to the *pub*lic, hmm?'

James maintained his silence.

Hamish started to pace again. 'A-and you've probably been wondering all evening – why do I have those *awful* foreigners as house guests? Well, it's simply – and I have to be frank – it's because one can charge them a b-bloody fortune for a couple of days shooting, that's why.'

'But it's still not enough,' James deduced while Hamish drew breath, 'so the painting has to go, correct?'

Preoccupied, Hamish, picked up where he'd left off. 'I mean, dammit, father flogged off everything else of real value years ago. To cover business debts, back taxes, that sort of thing.' He tugged his earlobe while an afterthought formed. 'A-and, well, OK – booze and girlies too, you know. Hmm, plus a bit of gambling here and there, it has to be said.'

James suppressed a smile. 'But why keep the sale of the painting a secret? That way, you could lose out.'

Finally biting the bullet, Hamish stopped pacing again and faced James. 'I'm afraid you don't understand, old boy.' He went on to divulge – though with a definite hint of pique – that the castle, its contents, the entire estate belonged to a trust, as was common practice these days. He'd been told it was something to do with tax avoidance – or was it evasion? He wasn't sure. But he *was* sure that, if the existence of the painting became known to the trustees – damned bankers, lawyers and such – it would be curtains for him.

James nodded his head. 'You mean, they'd claim ownership of the lot, and auction it off to keep the creditors at bay.'

'Bull's eye, James. And it's a dead cert that I – I –'

'Would get sweet –'

'Fuck all, mate! Sweet f-fuck all!'

Although he fully recognised the seriousness of Hamish's plight, James found it impossible not to smile at the unrefined nature of his reaction. But he needn't have worried: Hamish was too caught up in the drama of his own unbosoming to have noticed.

'Dash it all, James, I'm only forty – still a young man, when all's said and done. I need company. I mean *fun* company. You know, back in London with one's chums, where – where one can really spend a few million in style. Damn right, i-instead of stuck up here with the – the –'

'Sheep?'

'A-absolutely. I mean, one isn't like one's father. I'm just not cut out to be your typical Highland laird.' Hamish gave that some thought for a couple of seconds. 'Well, not *yet* anyway.'

'OK, so you want me to find you a *secret* buyer for the painting, right?'

'Spot on, old boy!'

'Someone who'll never divulge that it exists, correct?'

'Brilliant – you've got it!'

James indicated the solitary chair facing the painting. 'Someone who'll keep it hidden away for his own exclusive enjoyment, the way your forebears did … luckily for you.'

'Hole in one!' Hamish canted his head, like a puppy waiting for a treat. 'Can do, matey?'

Deliberately leaving Hamish to hang on tenterhooks, James calmly returned to the painting and studied it at close quarters again. 'Mmm, really grimy,' he said after a while. 'It'll have to be cleaned before I can do anything for you.'

Hamish's jaw dropped. 'How? I mean … who? … where?'

James gave him a pat on the back. 'Relax, Hamish. Just leave everything to me.'

'And, um … a *buyer*?'

'Yes, yes, yes,' James crooned, as if calming a fretful child. 'Don't worry, I already have someone in mind.'

Hamish still didn't look entirely comfortable. 'But what about those Inland Revenue chappies? One wouldn't want them to get their greedy mitts on one's mazooma.'

'They'll never know. My clients all use tax havens for their business transactions. Offshore accounts in places like the Cayman Islands, Bermuda, the Bahamas.'

This put a smile on Hamish's lips. 'Bahamas, ay? Sounds good. After living up here in the frozen north, one would welcome an excuse for a t-tan top-up while checking the health of one's funds.' He winked and rubbed his forefinger and thumb together. 'And, um…?'

'And, yes,' James smiled, 'I'll get you three million … guaranteed!'

This statement sparked another spluttered obscenity out in the corridor, so loud that even Hamish regarded it as suspicious. Realising he'd blown it, Charlie slithered silently away from the door, then, after a few paces, turned and walked nonchalantly back, humming a sprightly tune. Hamish emerged from the room, looking apprehensive. But on seeing Charlie, his expression brightened and he swiftly shut the door behind him, leaving James to continue his viewing of the painting in private.

'Ah, Charles, fancy seeing you here,' Hamish grinned. 'What – I mean – where…?

Charlie slipped back into full-on fairy mode. 'Oh, hi there, Hamish. Fancy seeing you here as well. I was just, ehm … looking for the loo.'

'Oh, silly you!' Hamish scolded. 'You've over-shot by miles, a-actually. Come, let me point you in the right direction – if you'll pardon the expression. Hwaar! Hwaar! Hwaar!' Linking arms, Hamish started walking Charlie back along the corridor, but stopped after a few steps and looked him in the eye. 'Er, Charles, tell me – do you – do you shoot?'

'Pool or dice, love?'

That went straight over Hamish's head. 'No, I rather meant – tomorrow being the Glorious Twelfth and all that.'

Charlie responded with a deadpan stare.

Hamish tried again 'You know, the old grouse.'

Charlie didn't even blink.

'L-let me put it this way, and I hope you don't mind –'

'Any way you put it is fine by me, ducky.'

'What? Oh, yah, dashed witty, Charles.' Hamish forced an anxious little laugh. 'No, no, what I mean is, tomorrow, one wonders if perhaps you'd like to join us for...' He lifted an imaginary gun to his shoulder. '*Bang*! *Bang*!'

Charlie finally got the message, and he didn't like the sound of it. 'Oh, no, no, no! But absolutely no *way*!' He spread his arms. 'I mean, do me a favour – mess up my best leather duds? You must be bloody joking, darling!'

* * * * *

CHAPTER FIVE

*

THE NEXT DAY – A GROUSE MOOR ON STRATHSPORRAN ESTATE

* * * * *

Having to trudge across a mountainside at six in the morning, bollocks-deep in dew-soaked heather, wasn't an inconvenience Charlie had bargained for when formulating his master plan at dinner the previous evening. And it didn't help that he felt like a country cousin of Norman Wisdom's, kitted out in tweed plus fours that were several sizes too small, an equally tight shooting jacket, and a deerstalker cap that sat on his head like a dog turd on a pumpkin.

'Very fetching,' James said out of the corner of his mouth, though deliberately loud enough for Charlie to hear.

Charlie remained aloof, wondering why the hell he had allowed himself to be sweet-talked into wearing a set of hunting clobber that hadn't seen the light of day since Hamish's father was at boarding school. He was in the middle of a line of shooters, which included the male members of the current Strathsporran Castle guest list. James, appropriately attired and appearing totally at home in this environment, was positioned a few paces to his left, with Hamish, clearly out of his comfort zone, similarly placed to his right. Behind Hamish was old McClung, the tipsy piper from the night before, who had now assumed the guise of gamekeeper. Variously spaced along the line were the two Americans, the Japanese man and, out on a flank, the Italian duo, who had their upper bodies criss-crossed with cartridge belts and were armed with semi-automatic shot guns. Bruno and his *amico* were clearly not intending to take any prisoners. Ahead of the guns, a gang of Springer Spaniels was scurrying about manically, with a couple of black Labradors at old McClung's heel, looking as keenly confused as only Labs can.

'Not so many birds about this year,' James remarked to Hamish.

'No, it – um – it would appear not.'

McClung, nursing a hangover and feeling correspondingly less deferential towards his employer, glowered at the back of Hamish's head. 'No enough bein' spent on managin' the shoot,' he rasped. 'Simple as that!'

Hamish glanced over his shoulder, cupped a hand to his mouth and whispered, 'I say, McClung – decorum! Think of the paying guests, what!' He then adopted an affable air and smiled across at Charlie. 'Getting to grips with that double-barrel now, a-are you, Charles?'

Under such testing circumstances, Charlie was struggling to maintain his effeminate front. But needs must. 'Oh, yes, yes, just hunky-dory, thanks,' he lisped. Then, grimacing, he tugged discreetly at his crotch and mumbled, 'Not as much as this fuckin' Harris Tweed's gettin' to grips wi' ma knackers, but!'

Muttering to himself, old McClung glared at Charlie and Hamish in turn. 'Damn pansies, pollutin' the heather! Aye, it's no wonder the grouses is desertin' in droves these days!'

Suddenly, the dogs flushed out a covey of birds, which came whirring over the moor towards the line. One grouse veered off and flew directly towards the two Italians, who went into a frenzy of excitement, opening up with a rapid-fire fusillade that blasted their target into a mid-air explosion of feathers. Delighted, the two sportsmen indulged themselves in an animated exchange of congratulations…

'Ay-y-y-y! *Bravo, amic*! *Bravo*!'

'*Si, si, un colpo buonissimo, eh*!'

'My God,' McClung lamented, 'I fear for the bloody butterfies next!'

Meantime, the rest of the shooting party had failed to bag a single bird, with the exception of James, who had brought down a brace with one shot. His companions were quick to offer their praise…

'Wow! I say!' gasped Hamish.

'Way to go!' said Homer.

'Aye, fine shot, sir!' McClung concurred.

While James acknowledged their accolades with a modest smile, Virgil, Homer's American friend, stared wonderstruck at the fast-departing covey of surviving grouse…

'Yup, them little Scotch fellas is sure smarter than the average turkey!'

In contrast, Mr Harikoto was more interested in finding a reason for his disappointing show of marksmanship. He inspected his gun meticulously, then declared, 'So! Made-in-England … rubbish!'

It was then that Hamish noticed there was something more serious to be concerned about. 'I – I say,' he said, 'what on *earth* has become of Charles?'

McClung was quick to respond: 'Wi' any luck, somebody's shot the bugger!'

'Hey, do have a care, McClung! Let's have some, you know, a t-touch of respect, OK!'

A moment later, Charlie's head rose from the heather, his cap askew, a look of agony contorting his face.

'Well, he's still alive,' James observed, indifferently.

Charlie sat up, holding his left shoulder and groaning.

Hamish was all of a flutter. 'Good heavens, Charles, have you been…? I – I mean, are you –?'

'He's no been shot,' McClung butted in, 'if that's what's botherin' ye.' He took a hip flask from his pocket and unscrewed the top.

Hamish held out his hand. 'Ah, jolly good idea, McClung. Whisky – revive his ticker and all that.'

But McClung raised the flask to his own lips and quaffed a manly gulp or two. 'Ah told ye,' he burped, 'he's no been shot.' He indicated where Charlie was sitting. 'Look for yerself – no blood!'

Charlie quickly added an element of pathos to his fairy act. 'Yes, that's absolutely right,' he whimpered, 'it's because, the gun – well, it went and kicked me, that's what.'

'Ragin' bloody poofter!' McClung growled.

Hamish handed the old fellow his shotgun and rushed over to help Charlie up. 'Please – careful, Charles – let me...'

Charlie moaned as he attempted to struggle off his backside, still holding his left shoulder.

James arrived to lend a hand and immediately began to hitch Charlie upwards by the armpits, intentionally erring on the rough side of ham-fisted.

'Wa-a-a-a-ah!' Charlie yelled. 'Oh, hell – Jesus Christ – the pain!'

Hamish was working himself into a right state now. 'Whoa, steady on there, James! His shoulder – the recoil may have – really, you never know, it could be a-almost broken ... or something.'

While Hamish was faffing about, James took the opportunity to whisper into Charlie's ear: 'Wrong shoulder, Skidmark, You're right-handed, remember?'

Rumbled, Charlie had to think fast. The best form of defence being attack, he duly parried James's volley with a whisper of his own: 'Back off, pal! *Monarch o' the Glen*, right?'

This took the wind right out of James's sails. He hadn't seen *that* one coming. Stand-off number two – but this time the scales were tipped in Charlie's favour, and James knew it.

The other shooters began to mill around, wondering what all the fuss was about.

'He dislocate shoulder,' shouted Mr Harikoto, elbowing his way to the front of the crush. 'I fix … no problem!' He pushed Charlie's head forward with one hand, and raised the other in what appeared to be the prelude to a karate chop.

Charlie cowered, as did Hamish. James moved aside, giving Mr Harikoto space to deliver the blow. Then the two Americans waded in, grabbed the Japanese man and yanked him away. But Mr Harikoto fought back, displaying a surprisingly athletic mastery of the martial arts. This was beginning to look as if it could develop into something really nasty. The Italian duo took a few steps backwards, just in case.

'Hey, hey, cool it, boy!' barked Homer as he clamped Mr Harikoto in a head lock. 'Remember Pearl Harbour, huh!'

'Better believe it,' said Virgil, kneeing him in the groin. 'Who dares loses!'

Mr Harikoto was made of sterner stuff, though, and the struggle continued. Charlie, however, had been spared a broken neck and was back on his feet, smug in the knowledge that James was now in no position to blow his cover. He reckoned he'd been gifted a golden opportunity to get his master plan back on course, so his injury tantrums were suitably redoubled…

'Wa-a-a-ah!' he wailed again, one eye on Hamish. 'The agony! Treatment! Must get some … fast!'

Hamish put an arm round his shoulder, delicately. 'Fear not, Charles. I, uh, *we*'ll take care of you. Get you down to the village – a doctor.' In a spin, he instinctively appealed to the hired help. 'McClung – the Land Rover! C-carry him back to the Land Rover.'

McClung fired him a do-me-a-bloody-favour look.

'Now, l-listen here, McClung! I – I – I –'

With a benign smile, James stepped calmly into the breach. 'It's all right, Hamish, I'll take him. Mr McClung has a job to do here after all.'

Charlie didn't like the sound of this. 'No, no, it's OK, it's OK. I can make it back on my own – honest.'

'Who the hell are you kiddin'?' McClung snorted. 'Ye're in the Highlands, half way up Ben Doon, no sittin' in a poncey manicure parlour in Glasgow or somewhere like that!'

His conscience suddenly making its presence felt, Hamish then insisted that he should drive Charlie down to the village himself. James was quick to remind him, however, that he had a responsibility to make the day a pleasant experience for his shooting guests. He gestured towards the ongoing scrap between the representatives of America and Japan. 'Let's face it, you already have more than enough on your hands right here.'

'And he'll need all the help he can get,' Charlie chipped in, 'so just you stay here as well, Mr McCracken.'

In truth, Hamish would rather have been anywhere but on a bleak Scottish moor, and the chance to use Charlie's injury as an excuse to absent himself appealed strongly. But he was obliged to accept, albeit reluctantly, that James was right. There were times when one's upper lip had to be stiffened, and this was one of them.

'You're exceptionally brave,' he told Charlie. 'But James is correct, a-and I insist that he goes with you.' He handed James the keys to the Land Rover.

Charlie was about to object again, but was balked by the Japanese man, who wrenched a hand free from his wrestling rivals. 'Him – he!' he hollered, pointing menacingly at Charlie. 'He make wife poop pants in train already!'

James wasn't slow to realise that the scales of his stand-off with Charlie had just tipped back in his favour. 'What now, wise guy?' he muttered in his ear.

Discretion being the better part of valour, Charlie merely shrugged and limped off through the heather, with James providing willing support – ostensibly.

'Gosh, I do hope James will make it safely down, a-and back up again for us,' Hamish murmured. 'Jolly tricky track to follow … for the uninitiated.'

McClung took another swig from his flask. 'Aye,' he grunted, 'ye're no wrong there … sir!'

* * *

MEANWHILE – IN THE DINING HALL OF STRATHSPORRAN CASTLE

Senga the maid was busy dusting the furniture, singing to herself, her back to the door, when Farquharson entered, frowning. He was not a happy butler.

'Senga!'

Caught unawares, Senga spun round. 'Oh, hello again, Mr Farquharson. Turnin' out to be a nice day, eh?' She then resumed her work, though sensing an imminent dressing-down.

'And *what* exactly do you think you're doing?'

'Shaggin' Mick Jagger,' Senga said under her breath. 'What does it look like, ye puffed-up old fart?'

'Pardon?'

'Oh, just doin' the dustin', Mr Farquharson.'

'But I distinctly told you, first thing this morning, to polish the silverware.' Farquharson strode over to the display cabinet. 'Look at it! Disgusting state! This would never have been tolerated in the old laird's time. Mind you,' he huffed, 'we could afford *decent* staff back then.'

'Toffee-nosed old shite!' Senga mumbled.

'*What*?'

'Eh, nothin', sir. Just a wee sneeze. The dust, like.'

Farquharson extended his hand. 'Give me your keys.'

Pretending not to have heard, Senga returned to her work, humming as she dusted.

'Give me your keys – *now*!'

Senga's face was a picture of innocence. 'Ehm, what keys would that be, Mr Farquharson?'

'The keys to the silverware cabinet, of course!'

'Aye, well, ye see, Ah'm afraid there's a *slight* problem there.'

The butler glared at her, silently.

'Ah mean, what Ah'm tryin' to say is … could Ah maybe borrow your spare set for a wee while?'

'*What*!'

'Just till Ah find my own, like.'

Farquharson reacted as if he was going to have a seizure. 'You – you mean to say that you've *lost* your keys to the silverware cabinet?'

Senga lowered her eyes. 'Eh, that's cabin*ets* plural, by the way.'

'*What*! And the house full of … *foreigners*?'

'Yeah, but Ah'll likely find the keys easy enough,' Senga flannelled. 'Maybe Ah've only went and dropped them in the laundry basket. You know, with ma dirty knickers and that.'

Just as the butler was about to explode, Sarah, Lady Strathsporran, swept in, all twinset and tweed. Clearly in organisational mode, she homed in on Senga. 'Ah, Agnes, there you are. The very person I wanted to see.'

Senga smiled sweetly and curtsied.

Farquharson, quickly recovering his composure, bowed stiffly. 'Good morning, ma'am. I was just about to…'

Sarah brushed aside his toadying overture with a look, before resuming her address to Senga. 'Now, Agnes, would you –'

'Excuse me, your Ladyship, but ma name's *Senga*.'

'Yes, quite. Anyway, run along and help Hutchinson. He's driving some of the shooting party wives into Inverness. Shopping, or whatever. He, ah, they, um – they need someone to show – that is, someone who *knows* about shopping and such.'

'Well,' said Senga, making an effort not to appear too enthusiastic, 'if Mr Farquharson won't be needin' me, ma'am.'

'Ah, no, no, not at all,' the butler stammered, spitting razor blades. He cleared his throat. 'Just, uh, just do as her Ladyship wishes.'

Sarah shooed Senga away. 'Off you go then, Agnes. Hutchinson awaits.'

As she headed for the door, Senga gave Farquharson a cheeky little up-yours smile. His look left her in no doubt, however, that she was damned lucky to have been let off the hook. She'd get her comeuppance soon enough.

Unaware of this passing joust, Sarah wandered over to the window and stared out at the mountains. She was soon submerged in thought.

To remind her of his presence, Farquharson gave one of his butler-type coughs. 'A-*hum*! A beautiful morning, your Ladyship, if I may say so.'

Without bothering to look round, Sarah remarked that, while it was indeed beautiful where they were, a mist had started to creep down from the summit of Ben Doon. It concerned her somewhat.

Farquharson moved over to her side and followed her gaze. 'Ah yes, ma'am, but I shouldn't worry. McClung knows that mountain intimately – the quirks of the weather and so on. Yes, if he thinks the mist is likely to close in, he'll bring his Lordship and his guests down in good time, never fear.'

* * *

MEANWHILE – BACK ON THE MOUNTAINSIDE

It was all James could do to keep control of the ancient Land Rover. Even with the benefit of reliable steering, it would have been a struggle to negotiate a smooth way down the flank of the mountain between the rocks, boulders, screes and landslides that appeared round every twist and turn in what was more an obstacle course than a track. On one side, the ground fell away sharply into a gully, an unnerving detail of which James was acutely aware. To make matters even worse, he was having to endure the continual griping of Charlie in the front passenger's seat.

'Just gimme ma hundred quid back, ye thievin' chancer!'

'That's rich,' said James.

'*And* ma watch! Rolex Oyster – cost a bloody fortune!'

'Yeah, and this clapped-out old crate's a Formula One Ferrari! Rolex Oyster? Hah! I've seen better fakes on a hoopla stall.'

'Ah! So, you admit ye nicked it offa me back in the Edinburgh train station!'

'I'm admitting nothing. Just saw it clinging to your wrist like some silver-painted growth. Couldn't miss it!'

'Oh, ha-bloody-ha! *Very* funny! But more to the point, what's your real game anyway?'

'Game?'

'Aye, all this hobnobbin' wi' the gentry stuff. Come on – who the hell are ye tryin' to kid, eh?'

'Meaning?'

'Meanin', anybody that can dip pockets and snaffle wristwatches as slick as you is no fuckin' gentleman!'

James shook his head. 'I *honestly* don't know what the blazes you're talking about.'

Just then, the Land Rover slipped into a deep rut, throwing Charlie against the door. 'Oy! Look where ye're goin', for Christ's sake!'

James laughed. 'What, worried about your injured shoulder … *Charles?'*

Charlie opted to ignore that dig, but James knew he had him where he wanted him…

'Charles, huh? *Or*, more accurately, Charlie. That's Charlie Callaghan, or Sked, or Smith, even. Yes, and now it's Charles – Charles *Skidmore*, of all the silly handles!'

Frowning, Charlie glared at him. 'Here, you a bastard cop or somethin'? Right – lemme outta this thing!' He lunged over and tried to grab the steering wheel.

James shoved him away, propelling him against the door again. 'That why you faked the hurt shoulder, Charlie? Back down the castle for a bit of petty larceny while there's hardly anybody about. That it, Charlie?'

But Charlie was having none of it. 'Petty larceny?' he scoffed. 'Oh aye, is that what ye call the scam ye're gonna help yer mate Hamish with? *Is* it, eh? *Monarch o' the Glen*, eh? Well, Mr Smartarse McCracken, ye're gonna cut *me* in for a slice o' *that* action. Yeah, or Ah blow the gaff, right?'

'A pity your brain isn't as well-developed as your evesdropping talents, Charlie. Believe me, you're out of your league!' James chuckled to himself, then took a sideways glance at Charlie's deerstalker cap. 'You really *are* as stupid as you look, aren't you?'

That did it. Charlie flipped. He made another grab for the steering wheel with one hand, while snatching the handbrake lever with the other. 'Callin' me stupid, ye snooty prat?'

'Gerroff!' James yelled. 'You'll have us over the side, you maniac!' He tried to push Charlie back, but there was nothing he could ultimately do but close his eyes and pray as the Land Rover slewed towards the gully, bounced over a rock and took off like a rust-bucket equivalent of Eddie the Eagle.

* * *

A LITTLE LATER – BACK UP ON THE GROUSE MOOR

A heavy mist had now descended, blanketing the moor under a grey haze. The shooting party, temporary differences settled, had been reorganised following Charlie and James's departure and were once again trudging through the heather in line abreast, shotguns at the ready. Old McClung, however, was becoming increasingly worried about the deteriorating weather conditions. He said so to Hamish, who immediately found himself panicking again...

'What do you mean? I mean, what can we –?'

'Hey, Dook!' Homer called over to him. 'How d'ya suppose we're gonna see the friggin' grouse? Got any night sights on ya?'

Hamish replied with his customary nervous titter.

McClung, as might be expected, displayed considerably more composure. 'Aye, we should've got the hell out o' here a while back – Land Rover or no Land Rover.'

Hamish checked his watch. 'Hmm, one would have thought James would have been back for us by now.'

McClung pooh-poohed that assumption. 'Forget it! No way a bloody townie like him could drive up Ben Doon through a pea-souper like this. More likely in the pub … if he's any sense. Nah, we'll have to abandon the shoot – get back home on Shanks's pony. And bloody smartly an' all.'

'Excellent thinking,' Hamish enthused. 'A-and you never know, we may *still* meet the Land Rover en route.'

McClung dismissed this as well. 'No chance! In any case, it'd take far too long to go on foot that way. Over yonder,' he said, pointing, 'there's a wee, narrow sheep track that follows a burn down the back o' the mountain. Ye have to watch yer step, but it'll take us into the village in half the time.' Without further ado, he fired a shot into the air. 'OK, gentlemen,' he shouted, 'empty your guns and follow me. Sport's over for today!'

*　*　*　*　*

CHAPTER SIX

*

MEANWHILE – SOMEWHERE LOWER DOWN THE MOUNTAIN

* * * * *

Scarcely visible through the mist, the old Land Rover was lying nose-down in a watery bog, its engine roaring, back wheels spinning. Charlie was in the bog, trying to push the Land Rover out. James was leaning out of the driver's window, shouting…

'Put your back into it, man! Shove!'

'What do ye think Ah'm doin',' Charlie shouted back, 'washin' ma bloody feet?'

'Well, shove *harder*, OK!'

'Look, just put the fuckin' thing in four-wheel drive,' Charlie puffed.

James did as instructed. Instantly, Charlie was drenched by a spray of muddy water shooting up from the front wheels. He stumbled backwards, tripped and ended up sitting waist-deep in the mire. The Land Rover hadn't budged an inch.

'Aw, Jesus wept!' he wailed. 'Ma arse is soakin'!'

James switched off the ignition and got out. 'Well,' he grinned, 'the Japanese woman might say that's poetic justice.'

'Maybe she would, but Ah'd rather be sittin' in a nice, warm Richard the Third on the train than baptisin' ma goolies in a freezin' cold swamp half way up Ben-bloody-whatsitsname!'

'To each is own,' said James, then hunkered down at the back of the Land Rover and peered underneath. 'Yeah, just as I thought – big rock wedged solid under the axle. We'll need a tow.'

'Oh aye, so we will!' Charlie snapped as he clambered out of the sludge. 'Well, just you relax and Ah'll wave down the first passin' breakdown truck!' He squelched up to James and raised a hand. 'Adiós, pal. Ah'm hoofin' it … on ma tod!'

James watched Charlie waddle off into the gloom. 'Hmm, and you may be some time,' he mused. His own instinct told him that the most sensible thing to do right now was to sit tight and wait, in the hope of being found by the shooting party on their way home. But, with visibility already poor and the light fading, they'd almost have to fall over him first. And, being realistic, he had to accept that he was probably too far from the track for that to be likely. Unless…

A distress beacon, that was it! He opened the Land Rover door again and switched on the hazard lights. A ray of hope, though with its limitations. What he had to bank on now was the old crate's battery not going flat before Hamish and company showed up.

'Anyway, think yourself lucky,' he told himself. 'Things could be worse.' Then he was struck by the realisation that it had suddenly become colder, and was guaranteed to get a helluva lot colder yet. How to keep warm, that would be his next problem. If he sat inside the Land Rover with the engine running and the heater on, he'd probably be asphyxiated, judging by the exhaust fumes he'd already noticed seeping up through the floor. Then fate stepped, or rather, blew in. A chilly breeze swirled over the ground, passing by as quickly as it had arrived, but dispersing the mist for just long enough to reveal a possible solution to his dilemma.

* * *

THE KITCHEN OF STRATHSPORRAN CASTLE – DUSK, THE SAME DAY

The flagstone floor of the castle's kitchen covered an area bigger than all the kitchens of half-a-dozen suburban semis put together. In times past it would have been the 'downstairs' heart of the castle, bustling with cooks, maids, porters, footmen, grooms, ploughboys and gardeners, and filled with the aromas of baking bread, simmering stews and bubbling broths. But now its very size was as much an anachronism as the long-redundant culinary paraphernalia that still adorned the walls and shelves, dust clinging to them like memories of better days. At one side of the room was a vast open hearth, big enough for spit-roasting a whole stag, but now reduced to accommodating nothing more majestic than a geriatric wood-burning Aga.

Sarah was alone, peering out of the window at the gathering murk. She sighed, shrugged, wandered over to the Aga, poured herself a coffee and sat down at the big wooden table.

'What an absolute drag,' she muttered. 'No-one with any *pizzazz* to speak to in this antediluvian dump. Quite frankly, it would drive one to drink.'

The door swung open and Hamish tottered in, bedraggled and exhausted. He hung his jacket on a hook and looked across at Sarah.

'Wow! What a complete b-bugger of a day!'

'Yes, I *was* getting rather worried, darling. Coffee?'

Hamish slumped down at the table. 'Mmm, ra-*ther*. Gasping for one.'

Sarah returned to the Aga. 'Bag many?'

'Hm? Er, no – not particularly.'

'Oh, marvellous!'

Hamish watched Sarah pouring his coffee, then said: 'Sorry to trouble, my dear, but do you – would you – I mean, is there a drop of brandy about? I'm chilled to the absolute bloody marrow.'

Sarah reached for a bottle on a shelf above the stove. 'Probably not exactly Napoleon, I suspect. Most likely some sort of rotgut that cook uses for her, well … cooking or whatever.'

'Excellent. Just, um – just pour a goodly gargle into my coffee, if you wouldn't mind.'

Sarah did as requested, took a look at the bottle, raised her shoulders and poured a nip into her own coffee as well. 'Mmm' she said, 'I expected you back earlier, actually. All that fog.'

'Mist, darling. We're in Scotland.'

'Tell me about it!' Sarah countered, sotto voce.

'Anyway, yes, a bit delayed. Had to foot-slog it down a sheep track. Bit of an ordeal, really. Took hours, a-actually.'

Sarah handed him his coffee and sat down. 'Had to leg it, ay? How horrid! Land Rover on the blink again, I take it?'

Hamish stared at her, astonishment writ large on his face. 'Don't you know? I mean – James – didn't he tell you a-about … *Charles*?'

'James? Charles?' Sarah took a sip of her fortified coffee. 'What on *earth* are you talking about, Hamish?'

'You mean – the Land Rover – they haven't been…?'

Sarah frowned at him over the rim of her mug. '*Been*? Been what?'

Suddenly realising the possible gravity of the situation, Hamish clapped a hand to his cheek…

'Oh, my *God*!'

* * *

MEANWHILE, BACK ON BEN DOON

In the eerie stillness, Charlie could hear nothing but the rasp of his own breathing and the accompanying plod of his footsteps. What's more, all he could see now was an enveloping shroud of grey, and even that was growing ever less visible with the onset of darkness. Dammit, he had experienced mists often enough before: he was from Glasgow, and that's what they call 'air' there. But this Highland stuff – hell, it was more like vaporised porridge. He was soaked to the skin, numb with cold, hungry, dead beat and, although trying not to admit it, beginning to get just a *wee* bit scared. Not that he hadn't been scared before either, but this was different: something akin to how an aeroplane pilot must feel when looping several loops in a cloud – unsure after a while what's up, down, left or right. Also, without his watch, Charlie couldn't tell how long he had been staggering about like this. He guessed several hours, although it seemed like days. And now he was starting to see things. Hallucinations. Spots. Yellow spots. Two of them. Blinking.

But wait a minute… He half closed his eyes. Maybe his mind wasn't playing tricks after all. Maybe that was a pedestrian crossing up ahead. Could he be approaching a road? Civilisation at long last? The possibility stiffened his resolve to survive this nightmare. He stumbled on and, sure enough, the intensity of the lights increased with every step. There really *was* something there. Then, out of the gloom, the ghostly form of the old Land Rover materialised, hazard lights flashing. Charlie flopped against its side, as dejected as he was knackered.

'Bugger it!' he groaned. 'Ah've been goin' round in a fuckin' circle!'

But any port in a storm. He climbed into the driver's seat and felt his way along the dashboard. 'Must start the engine – get the heater going!' He turned the ignition key, but the starting motor only wheezed, while the hazard lights dimmed, terminally. He turned the key again. 'Come on, for Christ's sake!' But this time the starting motor didn't even make a sound. 'Uh-oh, Charlie boy – ye're in the deep stuff now!'

The shivers that had been running through his body during his futile bid for deliverance now graduated into a full-blown attack of the shakes: goose pimples rising, knees knocking, teeth chattering, muscles seized by cramps, the works. He was also beginning to feel extremely drowsy. Charlie knew that falling asleep now would mean he'd probably never wake up. Hypothermia was setting in, and he had to fight it. But how? It would be suicidal to attempt another blind yomp through the heather, yet the only benefit of remaining inside the Land Rover might be that his corpse wouldn't be devoured by hyenas – or whatever man-eating creatures roamed this godforsaken wilderness.

Come what may, he had to keep his brain active – continue thinking – stay awake. And the first thing that came to mind was James McCracken. Where the hell had *he* disappeared to? No way would that tailor's dummy have had the guts to try and make his own way off the mountain. Nah, most likely the jammy git had been found by Lord Hamish and his band of gun-toting numpties and escorted back down to a slap-up feed in front of a roaring fire in the castle. The thought kindled enough animosity in Charlie to raise his temperature by a couple of vital degrees. Not for long, though. The tremors and spasms that were the calling cards of the Grim Reaper soon presented themselves again, but even more forcefully this time.

Charlie's eyelids felt like lead, and the more he tried to keep them open, the more he wanted to doze off. His head began to loll about and he started to have little dreams, each one lasting only a few seconds, but as vivid as could be. The first one found him tucking into a roast chicken (it might have been a grouse!) in front of a roaring fire in the castle, with James's head on the body of a dog, begging at his knee for scraps. The second featured a kilted embodiment of himself, fighting off a pride of lions (they could have been hyenas!) on a windswept moor. The third starred Senga the maid performing the Dance of the Seven Veils with a set of silver plates, while the next had Charlie floating along a tunnel with a soft light beckoning at the end. An aura of peace, well-being and goodwill prevailed. Although drifting rapidly into limbo, something in Charlie's subconscious was battling to keep him compos mentis – a contest which ended with a sharp blow to his temple. He came to with a start, seeing stars as his head bounced back off the steering wheel.

Charlie blinked and blinked, but those stars wouldn't go away. He shook his head and thumped it with the heel of his hand. This finally did the trick. Each thump extinguished one of the stars, until only one remained: a dim one, but none the less persistent for that. Then it became apparent that the lone star was shining at ground level, so it couldn't be a heavenly body. As befuddled as he was, Charlie decided that this phenomenon had to be investigated.

He scrambled out of the Land Rover and half staggered, half crawled towards the mysterious light, which was now appearing and disappearing with the eddying of the mist. But each time the light reappeared it seemed brighter, which galvanized Charlie's determination to struggle on. This was the second time within an hour he had 'seen the light', and although the first experience had turned out to be a bummer, he felt that 'where there was light there was hope' – or words to that effect.

As if to prove it, the image of a tiny cottage began to take shape in front of him, its hazy outline lit by the mist-reflected glow from a solitary window. At first, Charlie thought it must be a mirage, another trick being played by his mind. Warily, he reached out to touch the cottage door. But it wasn't a figment of his imagination – it was real! Inch-by-inch, he pushed the door open, his heart racing.

A gentleman of sophisticated mien was sitting by the fire. 'Doctor Livingstone, I presume?' he remarked, without bothering to look up from his book.

Charlie stood on the threshold, transfixed. 'What the...? How the...?'

'Shut the door, will you,' said James, still reading. 'You're letting in the cold.'

* * *

MEANWHILE, BACK IN THE CASTLE KITCHEN

Hamish and Sarah were still sitting at the table, Hamish on the phone, looking extremely worried, Sarah, at least one sheet to the wind, pouring another shot of cooking brandy into her coffee mug.

'A-and you're quite sure no-one has been treated in A&E for an injured shoulder?' Hamish's face fell as he listened to the voice on the other end of the phone. 'I see. Well, thank you anyway … Yes, yes indeed, I *have* already tried the local GPs.'

Sarah hiccuped. 'No luck, ay?'

But Hamish wasn't listening. 'Something dreadful must have happened,' he said to himself.

'Oh, shouldn't worry too much,' Sarah breezed. 'McClung's right – they're prob-prob'ly in the pub. You know – getting quietly stonkered.' She raised her mug. 'Here's to London and – and absent friends!' Her mood then degenerated from tiddly good-humour to maudlin self-pity. She started to sniffle. 'How I miss them all,' she blubbed. '*Des*perately!'

Hamish was still too lost in his own immediate worries to be interested. Having thought things through, he lifted the phone again and tapped in three numbers. 'Hello – yes – would you put me through to the mountain rescue chaps? … Location? Er, Strathsporran … Precisely? Well, up Ben Doon, a-actually.'

* * *

MEANWHILE, BACK ON THE MOUNTAINSIDE

The inside of the cottage consisted of just one small room, as basic as a stable, but with two threadbare armchairs placed either side of an open fire. A pile of peats was stacked against one wall, and on another, a shelf holding a few books and some simple kitchen utensils was set above a wobbly table and a couple of equally decrepit folding chairs. A paraffin storm lantern and a free-standing wooden cupboard completed the cottage's 'conveniences'. On the table was an array of sandwiches, pies, sausage rolls, a large vacuum flask, two bottles of wine and a one-litre bottle of whisky. A wicker hamper lay open underneath.

James, wine glass in hand, was sitting contentedly by the fire, as though enjoying the comforts of a gentlemen's club. Charlie was standing inside the door, shivering, water dripping from his ill-fitting clothes, his expression a fusion of misery and mystification.

'Little pieds-à-terre like this would have been shepherds' shelters in bygone times,' James said, matter-of-factly. 'Nowadays, climbers and hillwalkers call them their *bothies* – no-frills resting places – even somewhere to have a kip.' He gestured towards the cupboard. 'Always a few essentials squirrelled away to eat in an emergency as well. And, of course, they're expected to replace in kind anything they've used. All very civilised – *and* honest.'

Charlie glanced over at the spread of goodies on the table. 'Pull the other one, pal. That's the shooters' packed lunches and stuff. Nicked it out o' the Land Rover, didn't ye?'

'No,' James smirked, 'I had it flown in specially from Fortnum and Mason's while you were away on walkabout.'

'Oh, is that right?' Charlie came back, unimpressed by the wise crack. 'Yeah, yeah, everybody loves a smartarse!' Without saying another word, he padded over to the folding chairs and placed them in front of the fire. With shaking hands, he peeled off his sodden jacket and shirt and draped them over this makeshift clothes horse.

James pretended to continue reading, but noticed out of the corner of his eye that Charlie seemed surprisingly ill-at-ease. Which got him thinking that his striptease performance would have been comical, if there hadn't been a hint of poignancy about it too. James recalled that, from the moment he first set eyes on him in the train station bar, Charlie had struck him as a born loser, and nothing had happened since to persuade him otherwise. Yet, though obviously a two-bit common crook, there *was* something about this character that made him hard to dislike: not exactly a *loveable* rogue, but not a completely despicable one either. In fact, James couldn't help feeling a bit sorry for him as he stood there, naked to the waist and trembling, with more goose bumps on his skin than a roll of bubble wrap.

'You'd better get them *all* off, if you don't want to catch pneumonia – or worse.'

Charlie sneezed, spot on cue.

'Go on! Get 'em off!'

Keeping an eye on James, Charlie started to unbutton the flies of his drenched plus fours. 'Aye, and don't you go gettin' any funny ideas,' he muttered.

'Mm?' said James, absently.

'*You* know what Ah'm talkin' about. You bein' in the same clique as Lord Hamish and everything. Aye, bent as a rubber screwdriver, that creep.'

While Charlie took cover behind the chairs and proceeded to remove his lower garments, James kept up the appearance of reading. 'Bent as a rubber screwdriver, you say. Takes one to know one ... *Charles.*'

'Aw don't gimme that crap! The Charles bit's an act, and –'

'And a damned convincing one at that.' James glanced up from his book. 'So, don't *you* get any funny ideas ... luvvy!'

Charlie glowered at him, laid his plus fours and underpants over one of the chairs, then edged out from behind, covering his modesty with crossed hands.

James, only just managing to keep a straight face, nodded in the direction of the food hamper. 'There's a tablecloth in there.'

Charlie continued to eye James warily while sidling over to the table, then attempted to cover his bare arse with one hand as he bent over to rummage in the basket. He swiftly hauled out the tablecloth and wrapped it around his body. Ironically, the touch of the cool cloth brought on another attack of the shakes.

'I can hear your teeth rattling,' James said offhandedly. 'Pour yourself a whisky. Get the circulation going.'

Charlie didn't have to be told twice. He knocked back a dram, shuddered and wrinkled his nose. 'Ah-h-h, that was good!' While he was helping himself to another hit, the big vacuum flask caught his eye. 'Ehm-eh, what's in the Thermos, pal?'

'Scotch Broth. Thick enough to race spiders on.'

'That'll do me!' Things were starting to look brighter for Charlie. He scoffed a couple of sausage rolls while supping a mug of the hot soup, then swigged another dram to wash it all down. The improvement in his circulation brought about an urge to lighten up the atmosphere. While selecting a sandwich from the table, something occurred to him that appealed to his sense of humour. 'Here,' he sniggered, 'the shooters – they'd be a bit pissed off at missin' out on all this grub and bevvy, eh?'

James was pouring another glass of wine from a bottle by his chair. He cast Charlie a chastening look. 'Not as pissed off as they'll be if they're still up there waiting for the Land Rover to come back for them.'

Charlie hadn't thought of that. Now his conscience was bombarded by images of the awful plight the others might be in. And all because his master plan had been stymied by having to come on this bloody shoot. 'Holy shit!' he gasped. 'The poor buggers!'

* * *

MEANWHILE, BACK IN THE CASTLE KITCHEN

Hamish was now pacing the floor, distraught. Sarah, pie-eyed, was sitting slumped at the table, fondling the brandy bottle. 'Fan-fancy anurrah, Hamiss?' she enquired, then, as befitted a lady of her station, burped discreetly into the palm of her hand.

'What?' said Hamish, his mind on other matters. 'Oh – yes – uh – thanks. Large.'

Sarah, swaying a little on her chair, upended the bottle over a mug. After a lengthy pause, she leaned her elbow on the table, missed, and a single drop of brandy dripped from the bottle. 'Oops!' she said through a vacant smile. 'Oh dear … emp'y!'

Hamish stopped pacing and scowled at her. 'You mean … none *left*?'

'Nup … all finiss.'

'Damned useless staff! What *do* I pay them for?' Hamish did a complete three-sixty, looking vaguely upwards…

'*FARQUHARSON*!!!'

*　*　*　*　*

CHAPTER SEVEN

*

*LATER THE SAME EVENING – ON THE
SLOPES OF BEN DOON*

*   *   *   *   *

The Strathsporran Mountain Rescue vehicle came lurching up through the mist and stopped, its way blocked by a large boulder. Five men got out and their leader wasted no time in assessing the situation.

'That settles it, boys. No farther tonight. In any case, visibility's so bad now I'm not even sure where we are any more. Best idea is for you guys to do a sweep on foot with the dogs, and I'll stay here by the radio. Yeah, and I'll sound the horn every so often to give you a bearing, OK?'

*   *   *

BACK IN THE BOTHY, MEANWHILE

James was still sitting by the fire, sipping his drink and reading – an empty wine bottle lying by his chair, a half-empty one standing beside it. Although *he* seemed sober enough, Charlie did not. He was slouched in the chair opposite, with his tablecloth 'toga' in blissful disarray. Placed within easy reach on the floor was the one-litre bottle of whisky, which was now half-empty as well.

'So, eh – you a cop, right enough?'

James was too engrossed in his book to answer.

'What Ah mean is, them other names o' mine that ye said. Ye know, ma ayley … aylish. .. aylsey–'

'Aliases?' James suggested.

'Yeah, them. How – how'd ye know, like?'

'Oh, connections, connections.'

'Knew it! Fuckin' fuzz!'

James glanced up and shook his head. 'I'm no cop.'

'Hmm, so ye say.' Charlie sat blearily weighing James up for a bit, then said: 'How'd ye know Ah was gonna larthenize the cathle, then?'

'Say again.'

Charlie fired him a dirty look. 'You heard!'

James marked the place in his book and, with a long-suffering sigh, placed it on the floor beside the wine bottles. 'Because, Charlie, larceny's your game. You've got a record as long as –'

'Aye,' Charlie butted in, 'bloody good it is an' all!' He took a sip of his whisky, a smug little smile on his lips.

James reached for the wine bottle and casually topped up his glass. 'Which is why you've spent half your adult life in the slammer, I suppose?'

The smile disappeared from Charlie's face. He lowered his eyes. 'Matter o' luck, intit?'

'Oh yeah? That'd be the same luck that landed us in this mess. And think about it – where the hell would you have been if I hadn't switched on those hazard lights?'

'Ah'd've managed,' Charlie shrugged. 'Ah knew where Ah was goin'.'

'That's right! Going round in circles, lost in the clouds a couple of thousand feet up Ben Doon, with the mist dribbling out your breeks by the bucketful. Get real, Charlie – the only place you were going was Stiff City!'

'Aye, well, thanks for turnin' on the blinkers an' that,' Charlie mumbled, suitably put down and showing it.

They sat in silence for a while, staring at the fire, each thinking his own thoughts.

Eventually, Charlie gave a chuckle and said, 'Ben Doon.'

James raised a perturbed eyebrow. 'I *beg* your pardon?'

Charlie was grinning now. 'Ben Doon. Great name for a mountain belongin' to that Hamish guy.' He started to laugh. 'Bloody arse bandit! Aye, Ben Doon, right enough. No in front o' him, but, eh!

James allowed himself a wry smile, as silence descended once more upon the bothy.

A moment later, Charlie sat bolt upright, looking towards the window. 'What the hell was that?'

'What the hell was what?'

Charlie got up and walked unsteadily to the window. 'That noise. Sounded like a fog horn.'

'Yeah, up a mountain,' James scoffed. 'Ships that pass in the night.'

But Charlie wasn't to be put off. He peered into the milky void. 'See – there it goes again.'

'Aw, relax,' James yawned. 'It'll only be a sheep or something. Maybe a Highland cow, looking for its calf.'

Charlie was far from persuaded, though. 'Hmm, maybe … maybe.'

* * *

OUTSIDE ON THE MOUNTAIN, MEANWHILE

The leader of the rescue team was standing beside his vehicle, beaming its search light in a wide arc. But there was nothing to see beyond the surrounding blanket of fog. He reached through the window and sounded the horn, then stood for a few seconds, listening. Nothing. He shook his head and grabbed the radio mike…

'Mobile base to search party. What's the score, lads?'

The loudspeaker in the cab crackled to life. 'It's like trying to see through paint now. Getting worse by the minute. Seriously, it'll take a miracle to find anyone in this.'

'Yeah, OK. Come on back, boys. We'll head for home, get some rest and try again at first light. I'll contact HQ now – get them to let the folks at the castle know.'

* * *

LATER THAT NIGHT – BACK IN THE BOTHY

The contents of James and Charlie's respective bottles had diminished considerably, and even James was beginning to feel a mite 'mellow' now too. To add variety to what was turning out to be a long and increasingly boring night, he decided to put his book aside and amuse himself by giving Charlie a grilling.

'So, what's all this interior-designer-for-the-connoisseur baloney about?'

A woozy 'Eh?' and a one-eyed attempt at focusing was Charlie's response.

'What I'm asking is how a bottom division lag like you managed to get your foot in the likes of Hamish's upper crust door?'

Instead of being offended, Charlie reacted as if he'd just been paid a compliment. 'Aw, it's *easy*!' he crowed, before going on to claim that all you had to do was place an ad in *Town Meets Country* magazine, offering free estimates, low prices, excellent references and all that sort of bollocks. 'Oh, aye, a dead cert ye're gonna hook some skint aristo or other. Get yerself kitted out wi' the leather poofter gear… Bingo!'

'But, instead of sizing the place up for wallpaper, you're sussing it out for a rip-off, right?'

Charlie's self-satisfied grin said it all.

'I've got your number,' James went on. 'I watched you eyeing the display cabinet last night. The plan being to come back later, jemmy it open and swipe the family silver, correct?'

Now Charlie really *was* offended. 'Heh, heh! Less o' the jemmy stuff, if ye don't mind!' He reached over to the chair where his jacket was drying and produced Senga the maid's bunch of keys. 'The work o' a real pro,' he said smugly, '*and* Ah got a quick Donald Duck into the bargain!'

'So, I *was* right! That's what your injured-shoulder act was all about. And for nothing more valuable than a swag bag of crap you couldn't touch without getting verdigris poisoning. Brilliant!'

Again, Charlie showed no sign of being insulted. He pulled a couldn't-care-less shrug and contemplated his finger nails. 'Water under the bridge now, intit?'

James canted his head. 'What are you getting at?'

'*You* know – you and me – got bigger fish to fry. Or should Ah say … *Monarch o' the Glen* steaks, eh?'

'Hah! Don't kid yourself!' James laughed. 'Like I said before – you're way out of your league, son!'

Charlie pursed his lips and nodded his head, slowly. 'That's what *you* think … pal!'

* * *

MEANWHILE, BACK IN STRATHSPORRAN CASTLE

'Uh! – *phew*! – gosh! We'll just – just get her to the – uh! – bedroom,' Hamish grunted as he and Farquharson the butler neared the top of the stairs.

Sarah, legless, was dangling between the two men like a rag doll. She looked upwards into the butler's eyes – or thereabouts. 'Oh, ish you, Farfarsum! Worra – worra *you* doing here?'

Farquharson flashed her a fake smile and inclined his face away from her brandy-laced breath.

The trio crabbed their way along the corridor, then struggled into a bedroom, furnished, paradoxically, in sober Jacobean style. Without ceremony, Hamish and the butler dumped Sarah face-down on the four-poster bed, where she rolled over, arms and legs flailing. '*Wee-ee-ee-hoo-oo-oo*!' she whooped.

Farquharson stood tactfully back, averting his eyes from the sundry items of next week's washing Sarah was exhibiting. 'Will, ah-*hum*! – will there be anything else, sir?'

'No, we'll – I'll manage now, er…'

'Piz-pissed-za fart!' Sarah called out, beaming delightedly.

'Thank you, um, Farqhuarson,' Hamish continued, still breathless. 'That'll be all. So, yes, just – just c-carry on.'

'Yes, juss – juzz c-carry on, Fartingsum,' Sarah giggled, wallowing about on the bed like a puppet with its strings tangled.

'Inebriate tart!' Hamish muttered.

The butler performed his regulation bow and glided post-haste out of the room.

* * *

BACK IN THE BOTHY, MEANWHILE

James and Charlie's individual degrees of inebriation were progressing commensurate with the diminution of the contents of their respective bottles. While Charlie, looking distinctly morose, remained slumped in his chair,

James stood up, took a couple of peats from the pile and lobbed them onto the fire.

'Aye, it's all right for you,' Charlie droned. 'Ye've no idea what it's like, havin' to claw yer way up from Shit Street.'

James wandered over to the window and peered out into the nothingness. 'Seems you didn't claw hard enough, though.'

'Bollocks! Anyway, how can *you* talk? Ye've no idea. Nah, never had a chance, me. Ah mean, bein' adopted an' that.' Charlie lifted a corner of his 'toga' and blew his nose.

Sensing an entertaining interlude in the offing, James ambled back and stood by the hearth.

Charlie's eyes were glistening in the firelight. 'Mother – ma mother – dyin' when Ah was just five an' everything.'

James gave him a few moments to paddle in his little pool of nostalgia, then levered up the pathos level. 'And your father … what about him?'

'Him? Never knew the bugger.' Charlie dabbed the corner of an eye. 'Bolted the course when Ah was born!'

'You weren't the bonniest of babies, then?'

'Oh aye, very fuckin' funny!' Charlie bristled.

Then something stirred at the back of James's mind. He didn't know why, but he suddenly felt compelled to probe a bit further into Charlie's tale of woe…

'Incidentally, where are you from?'

'What – originally, like?'

'Yeah, when you were a kid.'

Charlie sipped his whisky and stared dreamily into the fire. 'Glasgow … as it happens.'

'Yeah, but *where*? Glasgow's a big place.'

'Oh, nowhere,' Charlie sighed. 'Nowhere somebody like you would know about, that's for sure.'

'Try me.'

Charlie looked up, his expression changing from wistful to puzzled. 'The old Gorbals, if ye must know. Aye, like Ah said, Shit Street.' When this drew no visible reaction, Charlie redirected his gaze towards the fire. He sat deep in thought for a minute, then said, as if to himself, 'It was OK, though. Rough, but kinda cosy.' He swallowed hard. 'Yeah, it was all right – when ma mother was...' Charlie gave a little cough and wiped his nose with the back of his hand.

James sat down again, picked up his glass of wine and silently watched Charlie mulling over his memories. 'What about siblings?' he said after a while.

'Who?'

'Brothers and sisters.'

'What about them?'

'Well, was it just you and your mother, or...?'

'Yes – Ah mean, no. Ye see, there was ma brother. Big brother. He was...' Charlie stifled a sob.

James completed his sentence for him. 'In the orphanage too – after your Mum died.'

Charlie was struggling to control his emotions. 'Never saw him again. Adopted by another family ... maybe. Don't know. Ah was too wee, ye see. Like, too young to understand. Only five.' He dipped his head, and a teardrop dripped from the end of his nose. 'Aye, and they never... nobody ever told me where he went, where they took him.' His chin quivering, Charlie sniffed up the welling sadness, then gulped it down. 'Bastards!' Feeling embarrassed at having revealed a side of his nature he had always kept concealed, Charlie hauled himself up from his seat and wobbled over to the window, where he took his turn at gazing into oblivion. He was making a real effort to pull himself together, yet his shoulders soon started to shake, followed by an unsuccessful attempt to disguise a sob as a sneeze…

'Fuckin' peat smoke! Or maybe Ah've caught a touch o' the pneumonia right enough.'

Once again, James decided to leave Charlie with his thoughts. Now, however, certain things were beginning to tug at the strings of his own memory: hazy pieces of a jigsaw that had been swirling in his mind like the mists on the other side of the bothy window.

'And it wasn't called Shit Street, was it?' he said quietly.

Charlie was still standing with his back to him, and either didn't hear or preferred to keep himself to himself.

James waited a few moments, then said, 'Kilpair Street – number thirty-six – top floor – left of the landing.'

Slowly, Charlie turned around, frowning. 'What did ye say there?'

James returned his frown with a smile. 'The two O'Brien boys – wee Charlie and –'

'That's right,' Charlie butted in. 'But wait a minute. How do *you*…?' The realisation of what might be was starting to dawn on him, though he still suspected James was only having him on. 'Thirty-six Kilpair Street, ye said. The two O'Brien boys.' His frown deepened. 'But what's that got to do wi' you?'

'Her name was Mary … Mary O'Brien. And still the prettiest face I've ever seen.' James paused to allow Charlie time to take this in. 'And I can remember – Princie, she called you – her own wee Bonnie Prince Charlie. Imagine that!' he chuckled. 'If only she could see you now, eh!'

Charlie stood staring at James, unable to stem the tears that had started to roll down his cheeks. 'Ye mean to say you're…?' He lowered his brows again. 'Nah, ye're pullin' ma leg.'

James was struggling to control his own emotions now. He shook his head, a lump rising in his throat.

'Jamie?' Charlie whispered. 'Big … *Jamie*?'

'Seems like it,' James grinned, then took a handkerchief from his pocket and dabbed his eyes. 'Yeah, and seems I can't stand peat smoke either!'

They stood looking at each other for a while, saying nothing, smiling through the tears.

James was first to break the silence. 'So, wee Charlie O'Brien – haven't you got a cuddle for me after all this time?'

Bashfulness was not a condition familiar to Charlie, so he found the attack that now hit him difficult to handle. All he could do was look up, down and sideways, like a baby bird that had fallen from its nest.

James spread his arms. 'Well, come *on*, then!'

Charlie stared at his feet, rolled his shoulders, then lunged forward and grasped his brother in a bear hug. 'Big Jamie.' he half-laughed, half-cried. 'Who'd have believed it? Ah mean, who'd have fuckin' be*lieved* it, eh?'

James patted his back. 'There, there, wee man. It'll be all right now. We'll show 'em, just you wait and see.'

* * *

MEANWHILE, BACK IN THE BEDROOM OF THE CASTLE

Hamish was in bed now, under the covers, on his back, wide awake and extremely unhappy. Sarah was sprawled on top of the quilt, still fully clothed, but with a moth-eaten fur coat thrown over her. She was facing away from Hamish, eyes closed, smiling and floating blissfully through the land of nod.

'I – I mean, dash it all, Sarah,' Hamish griped, 'this is no life for a ring-a-ding chap like me. You know, all this tweed and heather and shotguns and those *dread*fully vulgar Yanks and Eyeties a-and such.' He took a deep, courage-building breath. 'So, that's why I'm going to leave you. Yes, I – I'm going back to London. With Charles. Yes, with Charles – a fun chap like that. Someone who really knows where it's *at*. Do, um, do I make myself absolutely clear, my dear?'

No reply. Sarah was well out of it, happily dreaming her inebriate tart's dreams.

'Sarah! Sarah, a-are you listening?' Hamish nudged her. 'Sarah? I say!'

But Sarah could not be contacted. 'Mm-m-m-m,' she hummed, 'kiss me, James – fiercely!'

Just then, the phone on Hamish's bedside table rang.

'Hello … Yes, it is he … Crikey! How *dread*ful! … A-at *dawn*, you say? … Yes, I understand … Hmm, well, thank you anyway.' With a panic attack looming, Hamish slumped back against his pillow and raised a forearm to his brow. 'Gosh! Poor Charles!'

* * * * *

CHAPTER EIGHT

*

THE SAME NIGHT – BACK IN THE BOTHY ON BEN DOON

*   *   *   *   *

The euphoria of their unexpected reunion having subsided, James and Charlie were sitting once more by the fireside, feeling relaxed and reflective, each one keen to find out how life had treated the other during their long years of separation.

'So that was it,' said Charlie. 'Next thing Ah knew Ah was adopted by this Skidmore family. Ended up in a flat out in the Easterhouse council estate. Aye, and if Ah thought the Gorbals was rough… Easterhouse! Jeez, some place!'

'Yes,' James nodded, 'there *was* that old joke about them eating their own young out there.'

'Who told ye it was a joke?'

James acknowledged that caustic crack with a lopsided smile. 'Anyway, I take it that's where you learned to pick pockets, was it?'

Charlie's expression was a study in disbelief. 'You *kiddin*?'

'Only asking – only asking.'

'Nah, nah!' Charlie chortled, 'Naw, it was *you* that showed me the ropes!'

'Never!'

'Tellin' ye! At the Barras street market. Ah was only four or something – knee-high to a flea.' Charlie giggled at the memory. 'Aye, ye made me target the wee Glesca women – the wee dwarfy wifies wi' the low-slung shoppin' bags.' He slapped his knee and laughed. 'No remember?'

'God, I'd forgotten all about that,' James confessed.

'Aye, maybe, but that's what ye did.'

A mischievous glint lit James's eye. 'Aha, but looks like you didn't learn well *enough*!'

Charlie was about to turn all prickly, but the penny suddenly dropped. 'Oops! Ah see what ye mean – the train station bar. Mmm, no one o' ma best performances, Ah must admit.' He sat staring shamefaced at the floor. Then he saw the other side of the coin. 'But here! Now we're on the subject – what about ma watch and hundred quid?'

James looked him in the eye, deadpan. 'You keep on about that. But really, what do you want me to say?'

Charlie raised a conciliatory hand. 'It's OK – it's OK! Ye've shown me up, and Ah'm fine wi' that. The best man won, but just gimme ma watch and folders back, if ye don't mind.'

'Look,' James sighed, 'I wouldn't want to come across as being a cut above or anything, but…'

'But?'

'Well, dipping pockets and swiping watches off wrists… No offence, but I just don't *do* that sort of thing.'

Charlie could see that James was either telling the truth or was a bloody good liar. But then, even if he was a bloody good liar, which he probably was, he wouldn't lie to his new-found flesh and blood – surely. He scratched his cheek, thinking aloud. 'So, if it wasn't *you*, who else could've…?' Then he remembered the elderly woman bustling him out of her way in the railway station ticket office. In an instant, what little ego he had left was deflated like a slashed tyre. 'The sticky-fingered old hoor!' he growled. 'The dishonest, thievin', underhand, sleekit, deceitful old shite!'

James didn't ask. He returned prudently to the subject of Charlie's childhood. 'So, life in Easterhouse – pretty rough, you were saying.'

Charlie was concentrating on licking his wounds.

'Kinda tough for a young kid, was it?' James pressed.

'Talkin' about Easterhouse, are ye? Yeah, yeah, but better than bein' in the orphan home, Ah suppose. Just left to run wild, ye see. Gangs, fights – bloody jungle!' Charlie thought about that for a few moments. 'Aye, Ah was put on probation before Ah was seven – curfewed an' everything. Bastards said Ah was nickin' sweeties in the paper shop.'

'And you weren't?'

'No way! Fags, man!' Charlie awarded himself a pat on the back. 'Oh, aye – too fuckin' true!' Choosing not to notice James's slightly abashed reaction, he poured himself another whisky, settled back in his seat and proceeded to warm to his theme...

Probation had only been the start of it. In and out of trouble with the police, then his first stretch in borstal at the age of sixteen: the young hard case who couldn't wait to become old enough to be sent to a real jail – a *man*'s jail. 'Happened soon enough an' all,' Charlie recalled, with just a hint of remorse.

'Glasgow's Barlinnie clink,' James surmised. 'The old Bar-L. Hardly a walk in the park for a kid, huh?'

'No, although they had more wild animals in that place than Glasgow Zoo. So, credit where it's due,' Charlie smirked, 'ye learned a few good tricks as well.'

James sat without speaking for a while, trying to fit these new pieces into his old jigsaw puzzle. 'After the orphan home,' he eventually said, 'when we were split up, I used to lie awake at night, wondering what had happened to you. I asked the McCrackens often enough, but they never said. Maybe they didn't know. Anyway, after a while, I just stopped asking. Tried to forget.'

'The McCrackens – that who adopted you, was it?'

'Yeah. Maw and Paw. OK, that's what they *wanted* me to call them. I never did, though.'

'Didnae like them, eh?'

'Actually, I did. Well, put it this way – I didn't *dis*like them. I mean, they were OK – nice folk, doing their best for me, I guess. It's just that ... they weren't *my* folks. Hard to explain. But anyhow, *you* know what I mean.'

'Hmm. But what about money? That would've made a difference. Well off, were they?'

'Well off?' James shook his head. 'Nah, permanently skint. We lived in an old tenement flat down the Cowgate in Edinburgh. Cold water, no bath, outside bog – just like the Gorbals, but with delusions of poshness.'

'Aye, well,' Charlie shrugged, 'that's Edinburgh for ye.'

James couldn't help laughing. 'That's right – the old fur-coat-and-no-drawers syndrome. Always a pan loaf, never a plain. Keep up appearances. A new patch on the arse of your troosers every year, whether you need it or not. Yep, that's Edinburgh for you.'

Charlie was getting a bit confused. 'So how – Ah mean, ye seem to have done OK for yerself – so how did ye manage to…?'

'Claw *my* way out of Shit Street?'

'Yeah, that's what Ah'm wonderin' about.'

'First step was to run away from home. The usual – lied about my age and joined the army. Thought I'd get a gun to play with.' He winked at Charlie. 'You can take the laddie out of the Gorbals, but you cannae take the Gorbals out of the laddie, eh?'

'That's one up for you again. Ah never managed to get ma hands on a shooter.'

'Just as well too, if you ask me. But anyway, neither did I, as it turned out. No, a pair of drum sticks, that's what *I* got to play with.'

'*Drum* sticks?'

'Yeah, they put me in the pipe band, would you believe!'

'Hell, you must've been *right* pissed off! Talk about the sublime to the ridiculous!'

'No, no! It was good. I enjoyed it – once I knew what I was doing.'

'Ye're jokin'!'

'Deadly serious. No, if you want to be a drummer, you can't get a better grounding than in a good pipe band. Take my word for it. Anyhow, after a while, some of the guys in the military band – sax players and so on – asked me to play in a wee dance band they had. Whole new scene. Gigs in the officers' mess. Extra cash. Great!'

'*Now* Ah get it!' Charlie beamed. 'Officers' mess, eh? And that's how ye met chinless wonders like Hamish, right?'

'Yep. His old man was my Commanding Officer back then. Got to know that landed-gentry set pretty well. Made a point of it, in fact.'

Charlie was impressed, though still a mite confused. 'But what about all this art-expert stuff? Ah mean, don't tell me ye picked that up in the army too. Like, stand by yer Rembrandts, was it?'

'Well, no,' James laughed, 'but that's another story. You see, I was still young, footloose and fancy-free when I jacked in the army. Hooked on jazz by that time – thanks to those same boys in the dance band. So, soon as I was back in civvy street, I headed straight for London. The Fifties – jazz was really taking off in The Smoke.'

Charlie sat enthralled while James took him back almost forty years to the night he first descended the stairs of a steamy cellar club in Soho. The toe-tapping sound of a traditional jazz band drew him like a bear to a bee hive. And the resulting sting was to make a mark on him that would last for the rest of his life. Not that he realised this at the time, of course. All he was bothered about was elbowing his way through the mob of jiving customers and getting himself right up in front of the bandstand. But being so close to live music, the likes of which he had only ever heard on record, soon had him gripped by an irresistible urge. There was only one thing on his mind now: he *had* to play with that band.

'I kept pestering the leader, number after number after number, till he finally gave in – probably just to get rid of me. That said, the drummer was completely knackered, thrashing about all night in that sweat box, so he seemed happy enough to hand me his sticks, even if his mates weren't.'

'Whatever, divin' in at the deep end like that, ye must've had a right dose o' the jitters.'

'I suppose I would have, if I'd thought about it. But no, I was so caught up in the music and the atmosphere and the whole scene that I couldn't wait to have a go.'

Charlie was all ears. 'OK, so how *did* it go?'

James said he remembered as if it had been yesterday. The tune was *St Louis Blues*, which the bandleader kicked off at a slowish tempo, for the simple reason that he wouldn't have trusted a cocky young wannabe like him with anything more testing. This had been absolutely fine with James; he understood the leader's motive, and was quite content to concentrate on keeping a steady beat, booting the band along without any showboating. And his swinging style, combined with a natural ability to complement rather than compete with the other musicians, won him their nods of approval as the number progressed. Even the leader, who had been the wariest of them all, signalled him to take a four-bar drum break to lead the band into its final 'ride-out'.

That had been like Christmas coming early for James: a gift out of the blue to be grabbed with both hands. At the end of his allotted four bars, he took everyone by surprise by doubling up the tempo and launching himself into a storm of percussive fireworks. The other guys in the band were soon shouting their encouragement, while the audience stopped dancing and crowded round the stand. James was so smitten by the buzz that he kept his solo going for several minutes, building excitement with a display of all the drumming techniques he had developed since his inauspicious drafting into that army pipe band some six years earlier. 'It brought the house down – almost literally!'

'So, ye blew yer big chance?' Charlie quipped.

James feigned a moment of coyness. 'Well, in all modesty, I can only say that I must have done *some*thing right, because, a few days later, I was on the road as a professional musician. Yes, and with the very band I sat in with that night in Soho – the Mick Melvin Jazzmen.'

Charlie's mouth fell open. 'No chance! *Honest?*'

James indicated the affirmative, which lit a light at the back of Charlie's memory store. He stared pop-eyed at James. 'Wait a minute … I remember you *now*!'

'You should do. I'm your bloody brother!'

'No, no – before – after – Ah mean back then, wi' the Mick Melvin outfit. Ah was only a youngster, but Ah can remember. Yeah, and you were Big Jim Mack, weren't ye? Had longer hair and a beard. Ace drummer. Played wi' Randall and Humph and Barber and, and –'

'And yes, I know,' said James with an unassuming lift of his shoulders, 'other bands too numerous to mention,'

'Yeah, topped the drummers' section in the *Melody Maker* poll for years, didn't ye?' Charlie's cup of adulation was overflowing. 'Bugger me! And all that time Ah was buyin' records featurin' ma big brother!'

James was the epitome of restraint. 'So, know a bit about jazz, do you, Charlie?'

'No – aye – well – yes,' Charlie stammered, overcome by a feeling of inferiority in such exalted company. 'Ah mean, Ah played maself, like – once – a wee bit.'

James made a tell-me-more gesture.

Charlie immediately wished he had never mentioned it. 'Banjo,' he said, almost apologetically. 'Or a fryin' pan wi' strings, you'd likely call it.'

'Not at all,' James replied, and if he was being less than sincere, he was doing a fine job of disguising the fact. 'An unjustly maligned instrument, the old banjo, I always say. Yeah, and I've played with some great players, like, um, well, Lonnie Donegan and, uh…'

'Don't forget Billy Connolly,' Charlie chipped in, and it was obvious that he certainly *was* being sincere.

'Yes, everybody loves a banjo,' said James, resisting the temptation to add the oft-used musicians' barb: 'from a safe distance.' He thought it more appropriate to ask Charlie how he had happened to follow in such august footsteps.

His diffidence sufficiently quelled, Charlie disclosed that one Paddy Feeny, an old lifer in Barlinnie, had given him lessons during his first 'stretch'. 'Sort of Irish folksy style, ye know. Good, though. Yeah, I liked that stuff. Then jazz – the Trad boom. I played wi' a couple o' bands around Glasgow. OK, not up to your standard, of course – but, yeah, Ah liked that an' all.'

'Well, well!' James grinned. 'Music's thicker than water, huh?'

Charlie was still struggling to come to terms with all of this. 'Jesus Christ!' he gasped. 'Imagine the famous Big Jim Mack bein' *my* brother!'

'Ah, but that was a long, long time ago,' James sighed. 'Yes, as Sam Goldwyn said, a lot of water's been passed since then.'

Charlie wasn't really listening. 'Let's face it, though – ye were magic. Top man on the skins. World class. So, Ah mean, why did ye stop playin', like?'

'Well, firstly, the whole jazz thing took a hammering when the Beatles came along.'

'Aye, Ah know,' said Charlie with a rueful shake of his head. 'Ah was there.'

'Anyway, long story short, I ended up going on the boats.'

'Cruise liners, ye mean?'

'Yeah – out of New York – the Caribbean run mainly. Playing waltzes and slow foxtrots for the blue rinse brigade.' James grimaced. 'Hmm, stuck it for three *long* years.'

'Nice gig, pity about the music, eh?'

'Putting it mildly. Mind you, I did make a few good connections for the art-dealing caper.'

'That's right – ye were gonna tell me how ye got into that.'

'Back to jazz and that first band I joined in London. The Mick Melvin crew. They had a singer – eccentric bloke called "Gentleman" Jonny Melba.'

'Yeah, Ah remember him. Bit o' a wild man, wasn't he?'

'So was the whole band, truth to tell. You wouldn't believe the shenanigans those guys got up to on the road. Bunch of first-division ravers. All booze-fuelled, of course. No kidding, it was a baptism of fire for a wet-behind-the-ears rookie like me. But I survived, and I learned a lot – not just about jazz and drinking either.'

'But ye mentioned "Gentleman" Jonny Melba. Where does he come into the picture?'

'Well, a wild man he may have been, but he was also a real art buff. Came from a well-to-do family, you see – privileged background, public school education, a proper toff, actually. Yeah,' James laughed, 'he used to say that, despite his start in life, he still managed to make his way up the social ladder to become a singer in Mick Melvin's band of musical reprobates.'

While Charlie listened intently, James went on to relate that, weird as it may sound for an itinerant jazz man, whatever city the band arrived in, old Jonny would slope off to the local art gallery while the rest of the guys were setting up the gear. For no particular reason, he talked James into joining him one day, and no-one was more surprised than James when he became hooked. After that, instead of playing poker during endless journeys in the band wagon, he would sit and devour books on art that 'Gentleman' Jonny had given him. 'Then he started taking me along to auctions, just to watch the fun.'

'Aye,' said Charlie, 'and big bucks changin' hands as well, no doubt!'

'There was that to it too – *really* big bucks sometimes. But anyway, without even trying, I made some useful connections in that game, and what with all the moneyed people I'd met in the army *and* through music in different countries, I started putting Tom in touch with Dick and Dick in touch with Harry whenever somebody wanted to sell a painting on the q.t.'

'Oh, aye,' Charlie winked, 'tax dodgers, like our man Hamish, eh?'

'None of my business,' James shrugged. 'I just take my fee – in cash – and keep the whole thing shtum.'

'Aha! And you swerve the tax man too!' Charlie's wink was loaded with admiration this time. 'Nice one, big brother! Good business!'

James said nothing.

For the next minute, Charlie sat pondering the things James had told him, wheels turning in his mind again. 'So, eh, if ye don't mine me askin',' he eventually ventured, 'just how loaded are ye, then?'

James clapped a hand to his heart. 'Loaded?' he laughed. '*Me*?'

For the second time that night, Charlie wondered if James was only having him on. And he sincerely hoped he was! 'But the expensive clobber,' he probed. 'Louis Whatsit suitcase an' everything…'

'Just a front. The essential props that come with the trade. Impress the clients – all that stuff.'

Charlie's sheepish smile did nothing to hide his disappointment.'Oh, Ah see. It's just … well, Ah thought that maybe –'

'Look, Charlie,' James cut in, 'I'm probably worse off than you. Right, you're skint, but I've got a list of debts as long as my arm. I mean, all this keeping up appearances – not cheap. OK, so I live in a nice London flat – St John's Wood – good address – but at the last count I was due the landlord over three grand in rent arrears. Me loaded? Hah! In my dreams!'

Charlie was visibly crestfallen. The golden image of his big brother had been all too quickly tarnished. Aye, he reflected, life really *was* a right fuckin' kick in the nuts at times!

* * * * *

CHAPTER NINE

*

THE CRACK OF DAWN – THE SAME BEDROOM
IN STRATHSPORRAN CASTLE

* * * * *

Hamish was asleep in bed, alone, but with the old fur coat which had been covering Sarah lying in a crumpled heap beside him. The clatter of the bathroom door jolted him from his slumbers. He sat up, rubbed his eyes, then frowned when he noticed his wife wasn't there.

'One can only hope she's sleep-walking into bloody Loch Ness,' he said to himself, 'although the resident monster won't welcome the competition!'

At that very moment, the sound of retching and vomiting emerged from the bathroom, quickly followed by the 'woosh!' of the toilet being flushed. Hamish glared at the bathroom door, turned his nose up and muttered, 'How utterly revolting!'

* * *

THE *OTHER* MONARCH OF THE GLEN

MEANWHILE, BACK UP BEN DOON

With the mist starting to disperse in the glow of dawn, a rosy bloom was filtering in through the bothy window. But James and Charlie were too taken up with their conversation to notice...

Charlie was still reluctant to believe that his big brother wasn't as flush as he'd assumed him to be. 'See, it's all a matter o' degree, intit? What Ah'm sayin' is, even if *you*'ve got debts, *your* debts'll be a lot less bother to *you* than *ma* empty pockets are to *me* – if ye catch ma drift.'

James's patience was becoming severely tested. 'Look, Charlie, hand-to-mouth, that's how I live. And I kid you not, it's becoming harder just to lay a hand on *any*thing these days, never mind put it in my mouth. Get it?'

Charlie did get it, though with reservations. 'OK, the way Ah see it is this – if things are *that* tight, ye'll be desperate to squeeze the best out o' this *Monarch o' the Glen* deal. Aye, and Ah'm thinkin' Ah might just be able to help ye there, by the way.'

James cast him a frosty look. 'Seriously, Charlie, if you do anything to screw that up, I'll personally strangle you – wee brother or no wee brother.'

Charlie raised both hands this time. 'No, no, Ah would never interfere. No way! No, it's just a wee idea Ah've got.' He hesitated, choosing his words carefully. 'So, ehm, what would be the, let's say, *commission* ye'd be expectin'?'

James assumed the air of a Mississippi gambler. 'Depends. Two ... maybe two-and-a-half percent.'

'*What*! Is that *all*?'

'You're living in dreamland,' James scoffed. 'Dealing with camel-wallopers and the like, it's difficult enough to get even that, believe me!'

Charlie wasn't impressed. 'Ye mean to say, if you earn three million quid for that spoilt ponce Hamish, all *you*'ll get out of it is a measly sixty grand or somethin'?' Now it was Charlie's turn to scoff. 'It's you that's livin' in dreamland, big brother! Yeah, Ah think ye should –'

'And *I* think you should shut your face, Charlie!' James was nettled and didn't try to hide the fact. 'To me, sixty grand is the difference between sinking and swimming right now. So, just butt out, OK?'

But Charlie was not to be so easily brushed aside. He smiled a shifty smile and tapped the side of his nose. 'Aha, but that's where yer lack o' a prison education lets ye down, Jamie boy. Now, why don't ye think about it *this* way…?'

* * *

At daybreak, the mountain rescue team were back on the job, following the same route, but finding conditions much less demanding, with only the occasional wisp of mist still lingering in the clefts and hollows of the mountainside. Even the spot where a boulder had blocked their way the night before proved easy enough to negotiate, and also seemed a logical place to resume their search. While his colleagues set off over the heather again, the team leader drove on slowly, heading up the track towards the area from where the two missing men had left the previous day. Unless they had attempted some seriously risky cross-country manoeuvres, their vehicle would surely be somewhere within sight – albeit lying upside-down in a ravine. He kept his eyes peeled. The first lead that presented itself, however, turned out to be less foreboding than a wrecked Land Rover. A thin ribbon of smoke was drifting up from behind a ridge several hundred feet higher up the mountain.

'The old shepherd's shack,' he murmured. 'I wonder…'

* * *

Back inside the bothy, the effects of a long, sleepless night were starting to show on James. Charlie, on the other hand, was on a high, buoyed up with enthusiasm for the second master plan he had conceived within two days. He was standing with his back to the fire, confidently addressing James, who sat stroking his chin, thinking, knitting his brows.

'Ah mean, if Hamish wants ye to *drive* the picture down to this piss artist in Edinburgh for a hush-hush clean-up, *and* says he'll lay on a van for ye to carry it in –'

'Nah, nah, it's not a matter of what *he* wants, Charlie. *I* don't want to let that painting out of my sight for one bloody second!'

'Not a problem. The main thing is the picture never reaches Edinburgh. Well, not officially anyway.'

'*Officially*?'

'Aye … according to the police. Know what Ah mean?'

'*Police*?' James screwed a finger into the side of his head. 'Have you gone completely nuts?'

Charlie tapped the side of his own head. 'Think Barlinnie, brother. Think bent. Play the game by *your* rules.'

James arched an apprehensive eyebrow.

Charlie could see that he still had a bit of work to do here. 'Fair enough, Ah can understand if ye maybe don't want to rip Hamish off. Ah always admire a man wi' ethics, like.'

James arched his other eyebrow. '*Eth*ics?'

Charlie ignored that. 'See, what Ah'm gettin' at is this… If ye do things *my* way, everybody wins, *no*body loses.' He raised both hands again. 'OK, OK, Ah know what ye're gonna say – the insurance company. But who the hell gives a shit about them? They're all bloody robbers anyway!'

As sceptical as he was, James reckoned there would be no harm in letting Charlie say his piece.

Charlie fully intended to in any case. 'It's a no-brainer,' he grinned. 'We fake a road accident, right?'

'A *road* accident?'

'Aye, yer van … it goes off the road!'

'Yeah, well, we've had some practice at *that*,' James mumbled, becoming more leery by the second.

Charlie chose not to hear that either. 'Along Loch Ness there,' he breezed. 'Scenery-viewin' place by the roadside. Kinda lay-by. Know where Ah mean?'

James shook his head.

'Anyway, it exists – take ma word for it. Ah had a slash in the bushes there on ma stroll from Inverness station the other day. Point is, though, a bloke passin' on a bike said the water in the loch's supposed to be bottomless there.'

'Yeah, right,' James pooh-poohed, 'it's *supposed* to be bottomless, but –'

'Listen,' Charlie interrupted, 'if it's deep enough to hide the fuckin' Loch Ness Monster for millions o' years, it's deep enough to hide a wee van for as long as *we*'ll need. Believe me!'

James heaved a weary sigh. 'OK, Charlie, tell me more – if it'll make you happy.'

'Tellin' ye, it'll be a piece o'cake. Just before you dump *your* van in the drink, Ah arrive in another van, do a switch wi' the painting, and buzz off, leavin' you to report the incident to the police.'

'An*oth*er van? How do you propose to come by that?'

'Obvious, intit? Ah'll hire one.'

'Oh yeah! And where will the money come from, if I may be so bold? And before you ask – it won't come from me!'

'Not a problem, brother, Not a problem.'

James closed his eyes and massaged his brow. 'So, to summarise… You want me to let you do the off with the painting, and –'

'And we meet up later – anywhere ye want, like – and you get on wi' floggin' the picture. Three million to us from yer donkey-walloper connection, and Hamish hits the insurance company for *his* three mil. Perfect!'

James pursed his lips. 'Hmm, the theory's there but –'

'But nothin'!' Charlie beamed. 'Trust me– Ahm yer brother, yer own flesh and blood'

'Yeah, that's what worries me.'

Charlie stepped over and gave James a hearty slap on the back. 'Ye have a grand sense o' humour, right enough,' he laughed. 'Now, here's what we do…'

* * *

THE CASTLE DINING HALL – A LITTLE LATER THAT MORNING

It was breakfast time, and all the remaining house guests were sitting at the table eating, with the exception of Homer the American and Mr Harikoto the Japanese man, who were at the sideboard, helping themselves to coffee and cereal respectively. Hamish slouched in, baggy-eyed and careworn.

'Good morning everyone,' he said, in tones that suggested he thought it was anything but.

Bruno the Italian was quick to greet him, in tones that suggested he thought it certainly was. 'Ay! *Ciao, signor duca*! *Buon giorno,* eh!'

Homer handed Hamish a cup from the sideboard. 'Yeah, good mornin', Dook. Say, what's the scoop on the two AWOL guys. Any nooz?'

'No, 'fraid not, a-actually. Yes, I, uh, just phoned the mountain rescue station, and their chaps are already back on the case. But, um, no – no news, a-actually.'

Homer looked concerned, but quickly put on a happy face. 'Hey, ya don't wanna fret too much, neighbour. Sure as fireworks on Fourth a' July, they'll show up sparklin'.

Yeah, thinkin' about it,' he chuckled, 'they most likely been partyin' all night on the contents a' that friggin' chow basket!'

Mr Harikoto tapped Hamish on the arm, scowling. 'He correct! Yes'day up mountain – no lunch, no transport like say in brochure! Want refund!'

This was the last thing Hamish needed to hear just then. His face depicted more pain than if he'd been on the receiving end of a Harikoto karate chop. But Homer, true to US Cavalry tradition, was swift to come to his aid…

'Hey, for Chrissakes lighten up,' he barked at the Japanese man, then grabbed his bowl and heaped it to overflowing with corn flakes. 'There ya go, bud. Now, just call it quits, OK!'

Mr Harikoto muttered grumpily in Japanese, shovelled an extra three spoonfuls of sugar onto his Kellogg's, shot Homer a triumphalist look, and stomped off to join the others at the table.

'Ay, *duca*,' Bruno called out, 'where ees-a your bee-oo-tiful-a wife? *Che bella donna*! The 'ow you say, flower of-a Scotland, *si*!'

'Quite,' said Hamish, then turned away, rolling his eyes ceilingward.

Upstairs in his bedroom, the curtains were still closed against the daylight. Sarah was on the bed, lying on her back, still fully clothed, a rumpled mess, a wet towel pressed to her forehead. She moaned bleakly, as only the living dead can.

* * *

MEANWHILE, BACK IN THE BOTHY

James and Charlie were slumped in their chairs in front of the dying embers of the fire. Both were sound asleep, their drink glasses, wine and whisky bottles on the floor by their sides, the remains of the shooting party's packed lunch on the table, the door ajar. Unknown to them, a sheep had strayed in and was standing in the middle of the room, gazing at them.

A few minutes later, a shadow fell across the floor as the leader of the mountain rescue team appeared in the doorway. He knocked, but neither James nor Charlie stirred. The sheep, however, turned her head. The team leader coughed loudly several times, and at last the two sleepers came to, blinking bleary eyes, squinting at his silhouette. He scanned the left-over food and empty bottles, noted the presence of the sheep, then did a double take at Charlie's dishevelled 'toga'.

'Having a bit of a party, were we, gentlemen?'

James and Charlie looked at the sheep, then at each other, speechless.

The sheep bleated.

'Don't worry, boys,' their rescuer winked, 'your secret's safe with me.' He stepped aside and beckoned. 'Now, if you'd care to come this way…'

* * *

THE CASTLE KITCHEN – LATER THE SAME DAY

Hamish and Charlie were standing looking at the wall above the Aga. Charlie, leather-clad again, had resumed his camp speech and demeanour. Hamish, for his part, was taking proceedings very seriously, though also seeming ill at ease.

'Chartreuse is the vibe I'm sensing,' Charlie twittered. 'Mmm, deffo chartreuse for the walls.'

'Chartreuse, ay?'

'Oh, no contest, luv! That against a delicate gamboge for the pine, I feel. Distressed, naturally, with…' He canted his head this way and that. '…yes, with some hand-stencilled fleurs-de-lys in alabaster on the cupboards. Mmm, nice!'

'Alabaster, ay? Gosh!'

'Oh yes, bang in vogue, the alabaster. Abso*lute*ly bona!'

While Charlie transferred his attention to the ceiling, Hamish was psyching himself up to say something significant. 'I – I say, Charles,' he began, nervously.

Charlie continued to contemplate the ceiling, silently.

'It's only…,' Hamish continued, hesitantly, 'it's only that I – I may not *act*ually be going ahead with the actual refurbishments – for the present, a-as it were.'

Charlie's eyes never left the object of his apparent ponderings. He folded one arm over the other and pressed a forefinger to his cheek. 'Mmm,' he pouted, 'ceiling's saying alabaster to me as well, you know.' Crossing his legs, he shifted his weight onto one hip, then adopted the akimbo position. 'I can see it now … pick up the tone from the fleurs-de-lys … muted, of course.' To add emphasis to his vision, he began to make a flamboyant gesture with his right arm, but stopped mid-sweep. '*Oo-ya*!' he grimaced, grasping his shoulder.

Hamish took the bait. 'Oh, my God, Charles – how distressing for you! I – I *do* wish you'd let me take you for an x-ray, or scan, or something of the s-sort.'

'No, no, it's quite all right. *Ouch*! It's only a bruise. Stiff – slightly stiff. Anyway, you were – *Aargh*! – going to – something about refurbishment?'

'Ah, yes, that.' Hamish stared at his feet and pulled an earlobe. 'Dashed disappointing for you, Charles, but, um, the truth is that one won't be proceeding as hoped … not in the immediate future, by the l-look of things.'

Charlie pretended to be more interested in kneading his injured shoulder.

But now that Hamish had started his unburdening, he felt empowered to continue. 'It's just that, well, I'm going away, you see. Back to London, and quite soon a-at that, I hope.' He gave one of his nervy titters. 'Yah, bit of a windfall coming my way, a-actually.'

Charlie pulled a shrug – a one-shouldered one. 'No probs, luv. A man's gotta do what a man's gotta do.'

'You mean, you're not – I mean, I haven't let you down, a-after all?'

Charlie was nonchalance personified. 'No, no – suits me, in fact. Yup, too much on at the moment anyway.'

'*Really*?'

'Yeah, yeah – absolutely no worries.' Charlie tweaked Hamish's cheek. 'Some other time … big boy!'

The reaction this provoked was a mix of relief and eager anticipation. 'Wow! Hey, magic, Charles! In that case, why don't we –?'

Under the circumstances, Sarah couldn't have chosen a more inopportune moment to make an appearance. Not in her husband's opinion at any rate. She stumbled into the kitchen, still wearing the same crumpled clothes, holding the top of her head with one hand, shading her eyes with the other. Death warmed up.

'Oh-h-h-h, Gaw-w-w-d!' she groaned.

Ironically, her timing couldn't have been better, as far as Charlie was concerned. While Hamish was being distracted by his wife's unseemly entrance, he grabbed the opportunity to take Senga the maid's bunch of keys from his pocket, place them on the floor, and deftly shove them with his foot between the side of the Aga and a box of logs.

'Sarah!' said Hamish in an embarrassed whisper. 'You *really* should –'

'Stop *SHOUTING*!' Sarah shouted. 'Can't you see I'm having one of my fucking migraines?' She staggered over to a cupboard, grabbed a glass, plopped in a couple of Alka Seltzers, veered over to the sink and half filled the glass with water. Without wasting a second, she retraced her steps to the cupboard, pulled out a bottle of gin and, hands trembling, topped up the glass.

As his wife took a long, luxurious slug of her curative cocktail, Hamish looked on in dismay. 'I mean, really,' he said to Charlie, 'can you a-actually blame one for wanting to cut loose from this?'

'Well, let's be fair,' Charlie replied impartially, 'a migraine *is* a pain in the arse.'

Sarah slumped down at the table and drew a bead on Hamish with one bloodshot eye. 'Cut loose? What do you mean, cut loose?'

'I told you, in bed last night. Damn it all, Sarah, it's hardly *my* fault if you were too pissed to hear.' Hamish tutted indignantly. 'Anyway, I – I'm leaving you.'

The kitchen was plunged in silence as Sarah stared at her husband. Her bottom lip began to quiver, tears welling in her eyes. She heaved a great, shuddering sigh and collapsed forward onto the table. 'Oh, my God, my God, my God,' she wailed into her glass of cure-all, 'I'm *so* unhappy!'

* * * * *

CHAPTER TEN

*

THE FOLLOWING MORNING –
STRATHSPORRAN CASTLE

* * * * *

Hamish and Charlie were standing inside the main entrance, chatting. A little cloud of despondency darkened the mood, and seemed to hover above Hamish's head in particular.

'Is there absolutely *noth*ing I can do to persuade you to stay just a t-*teentsy* bit longer, Charles?'

'Wish I could, luvvy, but like I said, a man's gotta do what a man's gotta do – and this one's gotta go and turn an honest buck, smartish.'

'Oh … I see,' said Hamish, wearing his heart on his sleeve like a black arm band. He stood head-drooped in pall-bearer mode, until disturbed by the butler arriving to announce that the chauffeur had the car ready and waiting to convey Mr Skidmore to the station.

Hamish was on the verge of tears. 'Gosh, Charles, it's been *so* marvellous.' He swallowed a whimper, then reached round and produced a wallet from his hip pocket. 'The, um, address of my pad in London,' he said, handing over a business card. 'Could you – I mean, *would* you…?

'Of course I will, you silly old nobleman! Next time I'm in The Smoke, I'll look you up. Mmm, can't wait.'

Charlie moved forward and they stood in a clinch, rubbing backs. Charlie's hand gradually ventured south until it arrived in the bum-groping zone, where it lingered, groping.

'Oo-oo-ooh!' Hamish cooed. '*I* can't wait either!'

While his hand was in the area, Charlie did what came naturally and whipped the wallet out of Hamish's hip pocket. 'Yes, well, too bad your windfall got in the way of things,' he said, prising himself free. 'But, hey-ho, as my old granny used to say, it's an ill windfall that blows *no*body any good, eh?'

'Sorry…? Oh, yah, now I get it. Wind-*fall*, ay? Hey, jolly droll, Charles! Hwaar! Hwaar! Hwaar!' But if there was ever such an oxymoron as a lugubrious laugh, Hamish had just provided a perfect example. All that was missing as he ushered Charlie down the stone steps were the strains of the *Dead March* from *Saul* being played on a pipe organ.

Not another word was exchanged. Charlie got into the back of the vintage Rolls Royce and sat smiling demurely, giving a queenly wave as the car glided off down the gravel drive. A minute later, Hamish's wallet, considerably thinner than before, flew from one of the Roller's rear windows and landed in a rhododendron bush.

* * *

Upstairs, James was in his bedroom packing, when there was a timid tap on the door. It creaked open to reveal Sarah standing in the corridor, still wearing the same crumpled clothes as the night before, her hair a tousled mess, her face lined with dribbles of mascara.

'What on *earth*'s happened?' James gasped.

'Oh, James,' she sniffled, 'I – I hardly slept a wink all night.'

He walked over and took her elbow. 'Come in, come in. Please let –'

'No, James,' she said, shaking her head vigorously. 'I know you're leaving today and...' She buried her face in her hands, sobbing quietly. '*Please* take me with you – get me away from here.'

This was a complication James really could have done without. Still, he couldn't just stand there and watch the woman working herself into a froth. He put a comforting arm round her shoulder. 'I'd like to help you, Sarah – honestly I would. But –'

'I'd pay you back my train fare, as soon as –'

'Look, it's not that, Sarah, I assure you. It's just ... well, I'm not even going by train,' he said strategically. 'You see, I've been asked by a client in Inverness to take a – a con*sign*ment to an art gallery down south, and Hamish has very kindly offered to lend me one of the estate's vehicles – a van – to transport it in.'

Sarah stopped crying, removed her hands from her face and stared at him with a look of utter disbelief. 'A *van*?'

'OK, it's a long story, but the fact of the matter, Sarah, is that I *have* to travel alone – for, ehm, for security reasons.'

Sarah inhaled stoically and tried to dredge up a modicum of aristocratic dignity, which was always going to be an uphill struggle when looking as if she'd spent the night in a ditch. All the more reason, though, to engage one's stiff upper lip. '*Do* forgive me. I shouldn't have imposed upon you like that. Yah, *terribly* bad form, I'm afraid.' She flicked her hair with an air of self-assurance. 'Not how one should treat one's guests. But I – I wanted to say goodbye here, in private, rather than…'

James nodded expectantly while Sarah blew her nose.

'Oh, James!' she howled in a flood of tears, her cloak of emotional control cast to the wind. She flung herself at him, throwing her arms around his neck, kissing him hungrily on the cheek.

James grimaced at the hum of booze oozing from her pores.

'Oh, James, James,' she warbled, 'if only, if only…' She gave him one final hug, released her hold, then turned away without making eye contact. 'Goodbye, James,' she whispered, and scuttled off down the hall, weeping.

James leaned back against the door frame and closed his eyes. 'Phew! That was a bloody close shave!'

Shortly afterwards, the butler came to collect James's suitcase. Although appearing a paragon of subservience as usual, Farquharson made a point of mentioning that, 'in the old laird's time', a junior footman would have been assigned the task of fetching a guest's equipage, but those lines of demarcation, like so many other principles of stately home service, were now sadly gone – as were all the footmen. James's immediate reaction was to tell the pretentious old prick that he was quite capable of carrying his own *equipage*, but suspected that this would only confirm the butler's opinion that he was nothing but a pretentious prick himself. Accordingly, he allowed him to carry his Louis Vuitton suitcase downstairs, and followed a few pretentious paces behind.

In the entrance hall, James found Hamish giving orders to two workmen who were lugging a large wooden crate. Hamish told them to lay it down carefully, and go outside to await further instructions. James was then greeted with what he took to be an attempt at disguising a less than relaxed state of mind.

'Ah, perfectly timed, James!' he said with a stiff smile, before turning to the butler and instructing him to instruct someone to fetch the van from the estate workshop. 'Yes, the foreman should have it ready by now, but tell whoever you send to make sure it has a full tank of juice. All right, Farquharson – c-carry on.' He then steered James across the hall and into the drawing room, where he immediately offered him a drink.

'No, no thanks all the same, Hamish.' James held up an imaginary steering wheel. 'Driving, remember?'

'Oh yes – yes of course.' Hamish made to tug one of his earlobes, but left his hand suspended in mid air, as if he wasn't sure what to do next. He finally opted for having a drink himself. 'Afraid I'm rather preoccupied this morning,' he admitted, while pouring a large whisky. 'Just one of those days, so please forgive me if I seem rather – you know, p-preoccupied.' He ambled over to the window and stared out, patently preoccupied.

James allowed a few moments to pass, wondering how best to handle what he sensed might be a change of heart on Hamish's part. He eventually decided to go straight for it: 'Look, Hamish, if you're not sure about this, we can leave the painting here. I can arrange for the restorer guy to come up and do the necessary in situ, and then I'll bring my client here to finalise the –'

Hamish wheeled round. 'No, no, no, absolutely not, James! Let the c-cat out of the bag, so to speak? No, that would *never* do!'

'OK, but seriously, if you're having second thoughts … well, there's always a way round everything,' said James, gambling on Hamish not calling his bluff.

'Dashed kind of you, but it's not so much the painting arrangement that's bugging me. No, it's just that there are, um, let's say *domestic* matters requiring my attention as well. Quite a lot on my mind, a-actually.'

'As long as you don't think I would do anything to –'

'No, no, I know you wouldn't, er…'

'Steal the Landseer?' James laughed.

Hamish laughed along valiantly, then succumbed to the weight of reality bearing down on his shoulders. 'Frankly, James, it's more important than ever that I convert the painting into hard dosh, a-and as soon as poss. Are you *sure* you'll get me the three million?'

James laid a hand on his shoulder. 'Surer than ever.' He crossed the fingers of his other hand behind his back. 'I'd bet my brother's life on it.'

'Brother, ay? Gosh, didn't know you had one, mate.'

'Just goes to show – you never know what surprises life's gonna throw at you.' While Hamish pondered the point, James pulled back his cuff and checked his watch. 'Well, time flies, and I've a long drive ahead of me. I guess the painting's in the box the two fellows were carrying when I came down the stairs, no?'

'Yes – absolutely. I supervised the crating myself, up the turret in father's glory hole, a-and everything's hunky-dory.'

'I'm sure it is, but – no offence – you don't mind if I have a look, do you? Can't be too careful with a rare work of art like that.'

'Oh, couldn't agree more, old chap. Couldn't agree more. In fact, I – I made them leave the lid unfixed for that very purpose.'

James was on the verge of being touched by Hamish's sense of fair play, but was prevented by the thought that he was up to his aristocratic neck in a plot to swindle his creditors, including the Inland Revenue. Nevertheless, this showed that, despite his apparent naivety, he deserved some credit for being prepared to have a go. By the same token, and while he reciprocated Hamish's trust wholeheartedly, no double-crosser likes to be double-crossed, so James returned to the entrance hall and had a good look inside the wooden crate.

'Yup, as you say,' he told Hamish, 'everything's hunky-dory. Nicely packed as well – professional job, really.'

'I say, how kind,' said Hamish with a coy little smile. 'Hmm, as I say, one supervised it oneself.'

The two workmen were duly recalled and told to screw the lid down.

While this was going on, James drew Hamish aside and said in confidential tones: 'Only one other thing, my friend – the provenance.'

'P-providence?' Hamish enquired, blankly.

'Well, we certainly don't want to tempt *that*, do we?' James chuckled. 'No, I mean the proof of origin, the painting's pedigree, the missive to your grandfather from old Queen Vicky.'

'Oh, wow, yah! Hey, almost forgot!' Hamish pulled said document from his breast pocket and handed it over.

James ran his eye over the letter, gave Hamish the thumbs up and tucked it safely inside his jacket.

A moment later, the butler wafted in. 'The van, your Lordship, is ready for Mr McCracken – fully filled with fuel, as per your instructions. I, ah-*hum*, took it upon myself to check the gauge personally, sir.'

'Very good, Farquharson. Splendid work.'

The butler dipped his head. 'Thank you, sir. Will there be anything else?'

Without replying, Hamish turned to the workmen. 'Now, chaps, if you've finished screwing, take the crate outside a-and await further instructions from Mr McCracken here.' He resumed his address to the butler. 'And you, Farquharson, if – um – if you would now show Mr McCracken to the vehicle...' He turned to James. 'I – I think I'll say *au revoir* here, old chum.' His lips began to tremble as he offered James his hand. 'Two sad farewells in one day ... t-two too many for me, I'm compelled to confess.'

James gave him a sympathetic little smile and a matching hug. 'I understand, Hamish. And thank you sincerely ... for *every*thing.'

* * *

OUTSIDE INVERNESS RAILWAY STATION, MEANWHILE

The old Rolls Royce rolled up and stopped at the kerb opposite the entrance. Charlie, carrying his scruffy holdall, got out, tipped his 'captain's' cap to the chauffeur and waved him goodbye. 'Right then, Charlie boy,' he grinned, 'first stop the self-drive-hire desk.'

* * *

LATER THE SAME MORNING – ON THE BANKS OF LOCH NESS

An ageing Ford Transit van, matching the condition of the Strathsporran estate's recently abandoned Land Rover, pulled into the deserted lay-by and stopped with its front wheels as close as possible to the side nearest the loch. There was no safely barrier. James, having first checked that the hand brake was firmly disengaged, climbed out of the driver's door and took in the scene. The view across the loch towards mountains stepping away to the horizon was truly breathtaking – as was the sheer drop into the water immediately below the van's front bumper. James's feeling of giddiness when glancing over the edge mingled with growing doubts about the wisdom of having agreed to go along with this scam of Charlie's.

His nerves on edge, he looked at his watch. Where the hell had Charlie got to? Then again, it could be a blessing in disguise if he didn't turn up at all. That way, James could revert to 'Plan A' and content himself with his sixty grand commission. Yeah, the more he thought about it, the more he hoped this would be how things panned out. He'd give it fifteen more minutes, then hit the road for Edinburgh – alone. Trouble was, this would be going back on his word to his wee brother, leaving him to cope with who knew what kind of jam he had got himself into now. What would their mother have thought of him treating his own flesh and blood in such a way? Spineless bloody Judas, no doubt! Yes, on second thoughts, he'd better give it *thirty* more minutes. In the meantime, he'd settle his nerves by checking that everything was as it should be with the painting.

He opened the back doors of the van and looked inside. Yup, everything seemed in order: exactly as it had been when the two workmen loaded the crate back at the castle. Four hay bales were propping it against the side of the van – an unconventional and, it could be said, somewhat crude method of securing such a valuable cargo, but an effective one nonetheless. Besides, it chimed with the rustic ambience pervading: sawdust and shards of bark on the floor suggesting the vehicle's association with the estate's sawmill, with sundry items of harness hanging on hooks and a heap of horse blankets at the back indicating equestrian connections as well. The latter also coincided perfectly, James mused, with certain aspects of Lady Sarah's appearance.

He was about to close the doors again when he heard the screech of tyres and the sound of a vehicle approaching at speed. A few seconds later, what appeared to be a brand new Ford Transit van hurtled round a bend in the road, swerved into the lay-by and skidded to a halt beside its dilapidated lookalike.

'I was beginning to think you'd decided to take a powder,' James told Charlie as he leapt out, grinning from ear to ear.

'Nah, just took a wee bit longer than expected to negotiate a deal for this van, that's all.'

'Tidy machine,' James said, dryly. 'How'd you manage to come by that, if you don't mind my asking?'

'Just like Ah told ye Ah would – Ah hired it!'

'What with? I didn't notice any rainbows touching down anywhere this morning.'

Charlie tapped the side of his nose in customary fashion. 'Ye could say it was a parting gift from that half-arsed plonker Hamish.'

'A *gift?*'

'OK, if ye insist – the truth is that his wallet *presented* itself to me, and Ah'm sayin' no more … except that Ah left his credit cards in it.'

'Well, that *was* big of you.'

'Forget it – Ah checked, and the dates were all expired, so Ah bunged it out o' the Roller.'

'Having first extracted the folding money, of course.'

'Telepathy, brother, telepathy,' Charlie winked. 'Thievery's thicker than water an' all, eh?'

James shook his head. 'I'm bound to say I don't approve of your way of looking at things, Charlie.'

'Aw, come on, man!' Charlie bristled. 'Ye knew we needed a second van, and Ah've got one, so don't gimme that holier-than-thou stuff! Anyway, more to the point, Ah presume ye've got poofy Hamish's painting in that old scrap heap there, have ye?'

James confirmed that he had, but his better self was whispering words of caution in his ear, and they were having an effect. 'Look, Charlie, I've been thinking carefully about this whole idea, and –'

'*Don't* fuckin' think! There's three million quid goin' a-beggin' here, and it's all ours for the takin'. What's to think about?' He strode round to the back of James's van and climbed inside. 'Right, gimme a hand to move this crate into the other van while the coast's clear. No, wait a minute – one small detail first…' He jumped out, took hold of James and wrestled him to the ground.

'What the hell do you think you're playing at?' James barked.

Charlie scooped up a handful of grit and began rubbing it into James's clothes. 'The master plan, remember? Brake failure. Convince the police ye jumped out just before the van nose-dived into the loch, right?'

'Yeah, but –'

'No buts! And while *you*'re givin' yer hard-luck story to the cops, *Ah*'m long gone wi' the painting.'

'Yeah, but that's *exactly* what I'm worried a– '

'BASTARDS! LOUSY FUCKING BASTARDS!' a woman's voice shrieked.

James and Charlie stared pop-eyed at the source of the outburst.

'Sarah?' James gasped, as Lady Strathsporran stumbled out of the back of his van, shedding her covering of horse blankets en route. She was sobbing with rage, and brandishing a mobile phone.

'How *could* you, James?'

'Hold on, Sarah – it's not what it seems. Nobody's going to lose. Just let me ex–'

'Shut up! You're nothing but common thieves!' Sarah punched some numbers into her phone. 'Police? … I'm reporting a robbery and kidnapping … The lakeside lay-by a mile outside Strathsporran village.'

'No, listen! Wait!' Charlie pleaded, moving towards her. 'Take it easy – it's only a wee prank we're playin' on Hamish.'

Sarah stepped back. 'Don't come near me, you obnoxious pervert!'

'Take care, Sarah!' James shouted. 'The hand brake – it isn't…'

But his warning came too late. As Charlie rushed forward, Sarah staggered backwards, bumped into the rear of the van and tipped it over the edge. Sarah went tumbling after, screaming.

'Jesus Christ!' Charlie groaned. 'The painting!'

Horror-struck, the two brothers rushed to the top of the cliff, peering over as first the van and then Sarah, still screaming, hit the water far below. Sarah disappeared instantly. They looked on while the van sank slowly, bubbles rising to the surface when it finally submerged. But there was still no sign of Sarah.

'Shit!' said Charlie. 'Now we're on a murder rap!'

After a few endless seconds, the crate appeared amid the bubbles, floating and bobbing like a rubber duck. James and Charlie could only stare down at it, dumbstruck. Then, when they feared the worst had happened to Sarah, her head emerged from the depths. Gasping for air, she grabbed hold of the crate.

'Thank God,' said James.

Charlie shook his head, flabbergasted. 'Look at it. Three million – the world's most expensive bloody life raft. Aye, a classless society, right enough!'

Sarah glared up at them, shaking her fist. 'BASTARDS!'

'That's *one* way of curing a hangover,' James observed with a wry smile, which was wiped from his face by the sound of a police siren in the distance.

'What now?' said Charlie.

They took another look at Sarah clinging to the crate.

'I'll get you for this, you poxy, low-life arseholes!' she yelled, still shaking her fist.

'Well,' James shrugged, 'I think that particular incarnation of the Loch Ness Monster is quite capable of looking after herself, don't you, Charlie?'

'You said it, brother. Now, let's get the hell outta here!'

* * * * *

EPILOGUE

*

A REMOTE HIGHLAND GLEN – THIRTY MINUTES LATER

* * * * *

Charlie's hired van was speeding along a single-track road between the mountains, with no other living creature in sight but the occasional scattering of disinterested sheep. James was driving, with Charlie in the passenger's seat.

'Last time we were sittin' together like this,' Charlie reflected, 'was comin' down Ben Doon in that clapped-out Land Rover.'

'Don't remind me,' James came back. 'Just make sure you don't freak out *this* time, that's all. Bad enough saying goodbye to my career as an art dealer, without being dragged out of a ditch by the cops and clapped in irons for the next few years.'

'Well, ye'd always have memories of yer Strathsporran adventure to look back on.'

'That's *all* I'd have! I mean, even my Louis Vuitton suitcase is at the bottom of bloody Loch Ness now.'

'Could be worse, though,' Charlie said, with a note of resignation that prompted James to cast him a look of total bewilderment. 'See, ye've got to look at it this way,' Charlie continued, gazing pensively at the passing scenery, 'ye've maybe lost yer slice o' three million smackers, but ye've found yer wee brother.'

James's immediate thoughts were along the lines of stopping the van and beating the shit out of his long-lost wee brother. But then he began to see the other side of the situation. Charlie was right. What was the point of crying over spilt milk – or, more accurately, of lamenting the loss of more money than he'd ever dreamed of getting his hands on? Nobody had been hurt – Sarah's dunking in Loch Ness and the damage to Hamish's faith in human nature aside – and he and Charlie had managed to snatch a head start on the police. In those respects they'd been lucky, and it was now all about making the best of a bad job.

'Ah'm gonna have to think about a way o' comin' by some more dosh,' Charlie sighed after a while. 'Ah'm completely skint again.'

'Nothing left of the dough you snatched out of Hamish's wallet?'

'Was barely enough in that to pay for the hire o' this van. Fact is, Ah had to negotiate a deal for a cash discount, and that's why Ah was a wee bit late arrivin' at the scene o' the accident – if ye'll pardon the expression.'

James started to chuckle.

'What's so funny?' Charlie snapped. 'Fat chance o' findin' a pocket to dip in this bloody wilderness. And Ah'm hardly best qualified for sheep rustlin'.'

'That wasn't a subject included in the Easterhouse curriculum, then?'

Such a daft notion made Charlie unable to resist a chuckle himself. 'Aye, bein' attacked by dope-heids' Staffies was the only experience o' livestock we had out there.'

James laughed out loud at that. 'Well, as you said, Charlie, things could be worse. We have to look on the bright side, don't we?'

'Aye, but bright sides cost, man, and Ah've no even got enough to buy a candle.'

James pulled a wad of notes from his inside pocket and passed it over to Charlie. 'This help a bit?'

Puzzled, Charlie gave the money a quick appraisal. 'Ah don't understand,' he frowned. 'Must be about a hundred quid here. What's the catch?'

James then produced something shiny from the same pocket and handed it to Charlie as well. 'Recognise this?'

Charlie's eyes opened wide, and a grin of Cheshire cat proportions spread over his face. 'It's – it's ma *Rolex*!'

James drove on, saying nothing, but smiling smugly.

'Ye foxy bugger!' Charlie muttered. 'Ye two-timin', double-dealin', pick-pocketin', lyin'-through-yer-teeth bloody fraud!'

'Couldn't have put it better myself,' said James. 'Yup, and all without the benefit of a Barlinnie education, by the way.'

Charlie was overcome by a medley of emotions, but the dominant one by far was admiration. With tears in his eyes, he reached across and gave James a hearty slap on the back. 'Big Jamie, big Jamie,' he gushed, 'Ah always *knew* ye'd make me proud one day. Aye, first ye turn out to be a drummin' star, and now this.' He stroked James's cheek with the back of his hand. 'Aw, big Jamie, ye've made yer wee brother pure, dead delighted, so ye have! Tellin' ye – pure, dead, fuckin' delighted!'

'Thanks, Charlie – I appreciate that, I really do. But maybe better save the celebrations until we've got ourselves out of this fix.'

Charlie looked over his shoulder. 'Hmm, Ah just hope we've got a big enough lead over the fuzz.'

'Well, I wouldn't worry *too* much about the Highland rozzers. They won't bother us where we're going.'

'Oh yeah? Where's that, then?'

'How's your sea legs?'

'Ah once went on a riverboat shuffle wi' a jazz band down the Clyde, and that's about it. Went as far as Rothesay, but Ah never spewed or nothin', though.'

'Great! That augurs really well.'

'Ye've lost me, man.'

'What instrument did you say you played again?'

'Banjo.'

'That's what I thought.' James pursed his lips. 'Mmm, could be a bit tricky for what I've got in mind.'

'Ah double on guitar these days an' all – if that helps, like.'

James's mien brightened instantly. 'Marvellous! Yeah, it's just that there isn't much call for banjos in the South China Sea.'

Charlie was totally bamboozled now. 'Ehm, geography's no really ma bag, but Ah'm guessin' that's a wee bit further away than where Rothesay's at, no?'

'Just a wee bit, Charlie, just a wee bit.'

Charlie ran a thumb over the edge of his wad. 'Accept Scottish bank notes there, do they?'

'That's probably where a few of those ones were printed,' James said. 'Very good at that sort of thing over there.'

'Ah'm likin' the sound o' this,' Charlie enthused. 'But, eh, what's the actual deal? A mean, Ah'll be perfectly honest wi' ye, Ah haven't a bloody clue what ye're on about.'

James patted his arm. 'OK, Charlie,' he laughed, 'I just wanted to check your reaction, but I won't keep you in suspense any longer. Here's what I've got in mind. You'll maybe remember I told you I'd once worked as a musician on the boats?'

'Of course – cruise liners – waltzes and foxtrots for the blue rinse brigade – out o' New York.'

'That's right. Well, I've always kept in touch with the agency that books the bands. Like I said, connections, connections – you never know when you'll need them.'

Charlie's eyes lit up. 'Now Ah get it! We're gonna be offski to New York, where the Highland polis will never catch us, right?'

'No, not *quite*, Charlie. Again, the theory's there, but the devil's in the detail. It's all about extradition agreements, you see.'

Charlie shook his head. 'Nah, ye've lost me again, big man.'

'It's simple, see? I get the agency to fix us a gig on one of the liners using China as a base. Shanghai's the best bet. They do the run down the East China Sea from there – Hong Kong, Vietnam, then over to Malaysia and so on. OK, there's still gonna be a warrant out for our arrest here, but that's the beauty of China – no extradition deal with the UK. Two or three years playing waltzes and foxtrots for the Brit tourists over there – just till the heat's off over here – and we're brand new. Yeah, and with a nice wee stash of tax-free spondoolicks in a Swiss bank account into the bargain.' James looked across at Charlie and cocked his head enquiringly. 'What think you of that, young Charlie O'Brien?'

'Will the cruise company pay the plane fares?'

'You bet. How many musicians could they recruit otherwise?'

'OK then, Ah think ye should step on the gas and get us to the nearest airport.' Charlie sat back and smiled at the prospect. 'Shanghai, eh? Aye, Ah do like a good vindaloo!'

'Well, um, that's actually Indian, Charlie. We're sort of talking Cantonese here.'

'Close enough for jazz, big Jamie O'Brien. Close enough for jazz.'

Brotherly laughter erupted and, as the van sped into the distance, a two-voice rendition of the Village People's *In The Navy* echoed through the glen.

A curlew 'wheeped', a lark trilled high above the heather, and sheep grazed indifferently on.

THE END

*If you enjoyed this book, you may also like the following
set-in-Scotland titles by Peter Kerr:*

*

'THISTLE SOUP'

- An Autobiographical Prequel to *Snowball Oranges* -

*"The story of his boyhood, a family and its farms.
Amusing, interesting, moving and true to-life."*

THE SCOTSMAN

"Kerr draws the reader into his vivid and fondly remembered past."

LIBRARY JOURNAL USA

"Beautifully written, gently humorous – a real gem of a book."

AMAZON UK

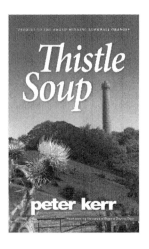

East Lothian is 'The Garden of Scotland' and the setting for this
delightfully idiosyncratic story of country life, from the time of
the Second World War onwards. Often hilarious, always heartfelt
and at times sad, this book will appeal, not only to those who are
interested in the Scotland of today, but also to people who recall,
or have been told about, rural ways that are gone for ever.

(Paperback ISBN 978-0-9573062-2-6)

(Kindle E-book ISBN 978-0-9574963-0-9)

'DON'T CALL ME CLYDE!'

- Jazz Journey of a Sixties Stomper -

(An Autobiographical 'Companion' to *Thistle Soup*)

"Laced with all the wit and eye for the telling detail one expects from this best-selling author. As intensely readable as it is enjoyable."

LONDON JAZZ NEWS

"Entertaining and intriguing, even if you're not into jazz."

TOUN CRYER MAGAZINE

"The story of a young man realising his dream of playing jazz for a living."

THE GLASGOW HERALD

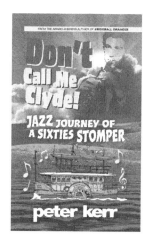

The Clyde Valley Stompers became, in the 1950s, Scotland's premier jazz band and first-ever super group. In 1961, at just twenty years of age, Peter 'Pete' Kerr inherited leadership of 'The Clydes' after they'd move their base from Glasgow to London. Despite many set-backs, the band stormed the charts the following year with their version of *Peter and the Wolf*, and were launched into the glitzy world of mainstream popular music. But, as Peter would discover to his cost, it was also a world tainted by greed. This is a story that will surprise and amuse in equal measure – and will occasionally shock too!

(Paperback ISBN 978-0-9576586-2-2)

(Kindle E-book ISBN 978-0-9576586-3-9)

'FIDDLER ON THE MAKE'

- *The Cuddyford Chronicles* -

"A hoot – pure fun – an observation on the absurd."
WELSH BOOKS COUNCIL

"A delicious, delightful and devilishly funny gem of a novel."
STORNOWAY GAZETTE

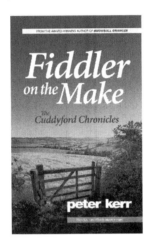

When the sleepy village of Cuddyford is colonised by well-heeled retirees and big-city commuters, Jigger McCloud, a jack-the-lad local farmer with a talent for playing the fiddle and an eye for the ladies, isn't slow to make a quick buck at their expense. Comic shenanigans, quirky characters and sinister ploys abound in this not-everyday story of country folk.

(Paperback ISBN 978-0-9576586-1-5)

(Kindle E-book ISBN 978-0-9574963-9-2)

'THE SPORRAN CONNECTION'

- *Bob Burns Investigates* -

"A really gripping page-turner that's peppered with laughs."
AMAZON UK

"Well off the wall ... escapist and liberally laced with humour."
EDINBURGH EVENING NEWS

The second in a trilogy of tongue-in-cheek Bob Burns mysteries finds
the droll Scots sleuth aided once again by the stunning, game-for-any-
thing forensic scientist Julie Bryson and keener-than-bright rookie
cop Andy Green. The action shifts from southern Scotland to Sicily,
New York and a remote Hebridean island, as the line between the
good and bad guys becomes increasingly blurred.

(Paperback ISBN 978-0-9573062-5-7)

(Kindle E-book ISBN 978-0-9574963-4-7)

*

Full details of all Peter Kerr's books are on his website:

www.peter-kerr.co.uk

Oasis-WERP

34033557R00086

Printed in Great Britain
by Amazon